"AJ, would you hold me?" she asked, but before the words had even fully left her, he pulled her into his arms.

There was the steady beating of her heart and the warmth of her breath on his skin. It had been so long since he had held a woman like this. A part of him wanted to take this so much further, to let themselves fall into the darkness of the night and let the shadows bring them reprieve from the stark illumination that came with the light of their truths; but ignoring reality didn't keep it from reappearing in the morning.

She leaned back slightly and pressed her lips against his. Their breaths mingled, mixing into a heady storm of want and fear. She broke their kiss, gently pushing him up to sitting. "I have to go, AJ."

MONTANA WILDERNESS PURSUIT

—————

DANICA WINTERS

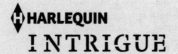

To my readers—I hope you have found an escape in
this world of secrets.

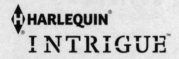

HARLEQUIN®
INTRIGUE™

Recycling programs
for this product may
not exist in your area.

ISBN-13: 978-1-335-58297-3

Montana Wilderness Pursuit

Copyright © 2022 by Danica Winters

For questions and comments about the quality of this book,
please contact us at CustomerService@Harlequin.com.

Harlequin Enterprises ULC
22 Adelaide St. West, 41st Floor
Toronto, Ontario M5H 4E3, Canada
www.Harlequin.com

Printed in U.S.A.

Danica Winters is a multiple-award-winning, bestselling author who writes books that grip readers with their ability to drive emotion through suspense and occasionally a touch of magic. When she's not working, she can be found in the wilds of Montana, testing her patience while she tries to hone her skills at various crafts—quilting, pottery and painting are not her areas of expertise. She believes the cup is neither half-full nor half-empty, but it better be filled with wine. Visit her website at danicawinters.net.

Books by Danica Winters

Harlequin Intrigue

STEALTH: Shadow Team

A Loaded Question
Rescue Mission: Secret Child
A Judge's Secrets
K-9 Recovery
Lone Wolf Bounty Hunter
Montana Wilderness Pursuit

Stealth

Hidden Truth
In His Sights
Her Assassin For Hire
Protective Operation

Mystery Christmas

Ms. Calculation
Mr. Serious
Mr. Taken
Ms. Demeanor

Visit the Author Profile page at Harlequin.com.

CAST OF CHARACTERS

AJ Spade—The highly trained military contractor and leader of the STEALTH Shadow team, who learns his past has caught up to him in the form of a son he didn't know he had and now must use every resource in his arsenal to find.

Amber Daniels—A game warden for the state of Montana who is following in the steps of her big brother and, in doing so, is learning to walk on her own in a world filled with danger.

Luca Fellini—A foreign minister of trade and the secret head of the now-defunct Rockwood corporation, who has ties to the theft of a variety of military secrets.

Frank Fellini—The son of Luca Fellini and a man who must choose to fall in line with his powerful father or find vengeance.

Charlie Reynolds—Tammy and AJ's two-year-old son, who has gone missing. AJ and Amber must work fast in order to make sure the boy doesn't succumb to the same fate as his mother.

Tammy Reynolds—AJ's ex-fiancée, whose remains are found near the STEALTH headquarters. With ties to the group, AJ must work with Amber to clear his name and find out the cause of her death before the team and its members are exposed.

Chapter One

Unlike people, bears weren't hard to understand. All a bear cared about was getting its next meal and not being screwed with—and maybe that was what Sergeant Amber Daniels loved most about the creatures. If asked, she would have been forced to admit—against her inner voice, which told her that to confess anything was to provide an enemy with ammunition—that she and bears were like kindred spirits.

Best part about a bear? They didn't have to take crap from anyone. For all intents and purposes, they were the top of the food chain and they didn't need to do a damn thing to prove their place. They were unquestionably the masters of their worlds.

It was a bear's power and natural brutality that kept people up at night. When it came to facing the truth that all humans were fragile in comparison to the masters of the forest—

regardless of who identified themselves as lambs or as wolves—this weakness turned to fear. And fear, well, *fear* turned into a need to control.

It was that fear and need for people to control that brought Amber to the field today. Trapping and moving bears was a major part of her role as a game warden in the state of Montana, but it always made her gut ache. With her affinity for bears, it was as if in trapping the regal animals, she was also trapping herself.

As much as she recognized the need to shake the thought and the weird attachment she felt to the animals, she constantly found herself thinking about certain bears she had trapped and moved in the past. Two weeks ago, she had been called to trap and tranquilize a nuisance black-bear boar who had taken up residence at a local apple orchard. The big boy had filled up on what was probably hundreds of pounds of apples before she had arrived, but all it took was the smoky scent of bacon to lure him into the steel trap laden with a bed of hay.

Black bears were entirely different beasts from the native grizzlies that roamed in Montana. A grizzly was unpredictable—docile one day and cantankerous and lethal the next. As much as she appreciated black bears, she equally feared the griz. The last time she'd run into one, it had bent the three-inch steel bars at the entrance of the bear trap she'd used to capture it. While trying to get the bear tranquilized in order for her and the biologist to do research on him, the big boar had reached through the bars and torn open her leg.

She ran the top of her foot over the still-healing lumps. If only she had moved faster.

The entire incident had cost her vacation time and, though she logically knew she shouldn't be, she had come away from the experience fearing the grizzly even more than ever before. Just seeing a picture of one made her heart race. No matter how much she attempted to talk herself down, a cold sweat would start to bead on her forehead. Luckily, in the two months since the accident, she hadn't been near another.

After the incident, she'd been forced to make statement after statement, as well as file a report with her superiors letting them know that she had, in essence, learned her lesson.

As for the trap, it had been so badly bent that her team at Fish, Wildlife and Parks, or FWP, had decided to no longer use gated steel bars and instead they were in the process of rebuilding their bear traps to have full-slide doors. The last thing any of them needed when they were unable to get cell-phone service and hours from civilization was to have a bear who had a leg up when it came to escaping a trap, or hurting one of the people tasked with working with them.

She made her way up to the front door of the Widow Maker Ranch. The place had grown immensely since the last time she had been here, but that had to have been at least ten years ago, when it still belonged to native Montanans.

She had done a little research, but hadn't heard much about the new owners beside the fact they mostly kept to themselves for the couple of years they had been there. In that way, they fit into the Montana culture even if they were transplants. Yet, it annoyed her that the first time she was meeting them, they were having a problem with the native wildlife. Why did people move to a state known for its feral tendencies and then want to get rid of the wild things the moment they were deemed inconvenient?

She tried to check her annoyance as she tapped on the front door. They hadn't called her here for her opinions. She just needed to do her job and get things set up to keep the bear safe. Hopefully it was nothing more than a black bear. If it wasn't…well, she wasn't sure if she was ready to deal with a grizzly. Yet, there was no one else to take the call even if it was a griz. She was one of only a handful of wardens in the state and they all had their hands full.

She could hear footsteps coming toward the front door. Hopefully these people weren't too talkative. She didn't want to play the ask-and-answer game that really only boiled down to the fact that they wanted the threat the bear posed eradicated.

There was the click of a lock opening, and she was surprised to find a thirtysomething man with a dimple in his chin answering the door. He looked her up and down, then glanced over her shoulder toward her dark silver forest-service truck with the Fish, Wildlife and Parks emblem on the door. If the guy knew anything about Montana, he would know who she was immediately based just on the color of her pickup. It was a specialty color designated just for people like her—people who never wanted to be noticed yet constantly were.

"You must be the game warden?" He sounded at odds with his assumption, as though he didn't think a woman could do the job. She disliked him already—that might have just about been a land speed record.

"Yeah, the name is Sergeant Daniels. I'm here with Montana Fish, Wildlife and Parks.

Someone called us about a nuisance bear?" Thankfully she was on her game, or she was sure that she would've given away her true feelings with a poorly timed eye roll by now.

The guy leaned against the doorframe as she noticed a collection of dirty boots and shoes just inside. There must have been at least thirty pairs. Clearly he wasn't the only one living here, but then she should have known that already. A ranch wasn't a place that could be controlled and managed by one person. To be an efficient and profitable ranch, which it appeared to be, people had to have entire teams to help with animals and the day-to-day operations.

She had grown up on a wheat farm on the east side of the state; and at some points of the year, her family had dozens of different people employed just to help with harvests. Often, she didn't even know all of their employees' names. Sometimes she missed those days.

"I was thinking I would take you out to where the bear's been seen quite a few times. It's close to the edge of our property. We're thinking he has plans on denning up there for the winter. With everything we have going on in the property, we think it's best if he just hits the road, you know?" The guy gave her a smile she was sure most women adored.

She found the action irritating, but she also couldn't help but wonder who was the other half of his "we." He was probably married—he was too handsome and charming to be single.

Though she was more than aware she was better off not speaking her mind, she couldn't help herself. "You know, sir, it is the policy of Fish, Wildlife and Parks to only remove animals that pose a significant risk to people and/or livestock. A bear who is merely being a bear, well…that's actually one of those things that should be expected. He hasn't been in your garbage or killed any livestock, has he?"

The man's smile rapidly disappeared. "Not exactly."

She should've kept her mouth shut. In cases like this, where she was called out to ranches with "nuisance bears" that were really doing nothing more than annoying the landowners, if she didn't act and remove the bears, the majestic creatures were often later found dead. Or they merely disappeared. There was an old rancher saying that went "shoot, shovel and shut up" in the state of Montana, and she was sure it happened more often than not when it came to these kinds of situations.

If she wanted to save the bear, this was her chance.

At least this man didn't know the old idiom,

or she probably would've never gotten the phone call. She just had to remind herself that she was removing a good bear from nuisance people. If she looked at it any other way, she wouldn't be able to keep doing this kind of work.

She forced herself to smile. "Yeah, why don't you show me where you've run into this bear? Let's see what we can get done here."

The man grabbed his jacket from a coatrack so full that its base had grown loose, making it list to the left, and the top was pressed against the wall. It made her wonder if it ever just gave up. The people who lived here were destroying everything they touched, even the things that were there to bring ease to their lives.

The coatrack teetered slightly as the man stepped by her, not even realizing the effects of his presence on the world around him and the potential for disaster that he so nonchalantly wielded. Not waiting for the rack to fall, she walked outside toward her truck. Her footfalls crunched louder than they had seemed to when she had made her way up to the house, but she wasn't sure whether it was her imagination, or if it had grown icier since she'd knocked on the door.

"You said your name was Amber, right?" he asked.

"I believe I said Sergeant Daniels." She sent

him a sideways glance. The man must have been doing a little research on her before she had stepped foot onto this property. It made a strange sense of foreboding fill her. "But, yes, my name is Amber."

"I'm AJ Spade."

"What do you do for a living, AJ?" she asked, motioning for him to get into the passenger side of her pickup. She sidled on around to the driver's side and got it started while she waited for him to get buckled in.

He stayed silent, like he was trying to decide what lie he was going to tell her.

"Obviously, and from what I've managed to pull about you, you are part of a club or something?" she asked, thinking about what limited information she had been able to glean from OnX maps and what little she had found on NCIC, the National Crime Information Center.

He smirked, but the little motion disappeared as quickly as it had arrived. "Yes, I'm part of a club. Actually, I'm the head of my group. We are kind of a subsidiary of the main club."

"What club is it?" she asked, more than curious thanks to the strange inflection in his tone.

He chewed on the inside of his cheek. "You are going to need to take the left turn up here, where the road forks. The bear has been crossing the river near the US Forest Service land back there," he added, pointing toward the mountain that abutted the back of the ranch.

She had asked him to point the way, but she had seen the maps and was familiar with the land and the river, but she let him treat her like she hadn't done her due diligence. Maybe he was used to working with people who walked into situations blind, but as a woman who worked in rural areas where people usually carried guns, she didn't take her safety or planning for granted.

"Do you have fruit trees back there?" It was a little late in the year for fruit, now that it had started to freeze, but if they had apples they could have gone to rot and brought in a bear that was getting ready for hibernation.

Usually, it was this time of year, right before bears went to den, they received most of their calls for bear removal as they would move into populated lands to find easy meals. Bears were at the peak time of hyperphagia—when they were trying to put on weight in preparation for hibernation. "We are pretty careful. Don't take our garbage out—in fact we burn it on site. Haven't seen the bear in that area. As far as fruit trees, I don't think we have anything besides just the normal hawthorns that grow throughout here. Haven't seen any berries for a while."

He shrugged. "I mean, we have tried to be careful not to draw any unwanted attention—from bears and the public."

Her intuition kicked into high gear. This man was hiding something from her, but as much as she wanted to press and get answers from him, it didn't matter. He could just go on hiding whatever it was that he wanted to hide. All she had to do was worry about saving a bear.

"How often have you seen the bear?"

He seemed to relax into his seat a bit more as she took the fork leading to the location he'd indicated. "It's been almost daily. The other night the dude even tried to break into one of the cabins tucked back into the woods. No one was living in it, and there wasn't any food, so we were pretty surprised."

"Bears have a damned good sense of smell— if he was going for a cabin there has to be something he wants in there." She shrugged, not wanting to start an argument while also making it clear that she didn't think any healthy bear was going to just randomly start attacking outbuildings.

"You're probably right," he said with a sigh. "We didn't have time to poke around the place a whole lot. We've been keeping pretty busy.

For all I know, there could be a cache of food or something."

She was glad he was willing to come her way at least a little bit. Maybe there was hope that they could actually work together in a positive way. It would make things easier if they could, but in the end, she would get the job done with or without his support and that thought brought her comfort. Validation was only welcome when it was used to pay for parking; the rest of the time she was good on her own.

"There is the place we have been seeing him." AJ pointed to the left of the truck toward the timber, where there was a small glen covered in a blanket of snow.

There were tracks all over, deer and elk from what she could make out from here, but she had no doubt that if she looked more closely, she would see the bear's. About a quarter a mile away and tucked back into the woods was a small cabin. It looked like an old miner's cabin. The logs that made up its walls were stained nearly black from years of harsh weather and the horsehair moss chinking someone had stuffed between the logs was slipping out from the cracks, giving the place what looked like brown dreadlocks.

"Was this the place he tried to get into?" she asked.

AJ nodded. "I'd be happy to show you the claw marks."

"You know if it was a grizzly or a black bear?"

If it was a black bear, it would be easy enough to trap or to bring in the bear hazing team and run it off from the property, but if it was a griz…well, they were far more temperamental. If it was one, she would be better off setting one of their large traps and getting up close and personal with the one thing she feared the most.

"It was brown." He shrugged. "I don't think I could actually tell you which one it was, for sure."

She pulled over and parked the truck between the cabin and the small little glen. "That's okay, most people can't, but I'll be able to tell by the prints." She waved her hand vaguely in the direction of where the tracks were. "If you want to wait in the truck, you're welcome to. I'm going to go take a look around." She made sure to give him an out if he wanted it. Most people were understandably not keen on the idea of rolling up on a bear hot spot with or without a game warden.

She got out, but took a quick glance in his

direction. He seemed to be weighing his options, but after a moment he unclicked his seat belt. She checked her smile as she closed the door behind herself and made her way toward the glen. There was definitely a large bull elk and a handful of deer that had moved through the area, but from the age of the tracks the last one had been through probably a week ago. Walking the edge of the snowy meadow, near the timberline, she found her first bear print.

The edges of the print were indistinct where the snow had melted and refrozen, but there was no denying it, thanks to the enormous spread and the claw marks—they were dealing with a demon with teeth, and she would soon have to face her fears.

Chapter Two

The woman who had been sent here to help him get rid of the damn bear definitely didn't like him, but he didn't blame her for her immediate disdain. He had found as a military contractor that most people didn't like him upon first meeting. They should have been glad—it meant that he wasn't sitting on the working end of a rifle scope that could have been pointing at them instead.

Sometimes the only separation between paradise and perdition was a little perspective—not that he would be anywhere close enough to this woman for her to ever even consider him as a source of happiness. They were just two strangers passing in the day, each to their own ends and requirements.

Though he was more than aware of their opposing goals and lifestyles, he couldn't help but admit that there was something in the way she looked at him that made him want to get to know her just a bit better. But it could have had something to do with the fact that she looked a little like the woman who had broken his heart.

There was a twitch at the corners of her cerulean blue eyes that made him wonder what had happened to her to make her look so angry, and at the same time, he wanted to be the one to fix her. That being said, he had more than enough broken pieces in his and his family's life—so much so, that he was having one hell of a time trying to bring the pieces together into some semblance of a manageable and functional organization.

The Shadow team, his family's private military contracting company, had taken a hit ever since they had grouped up underneath STEALTH and the Martin family...though that was through no fault of the Martins. It was just that ever since AJ and his siblings had formed the Shadow team, they had been taking one hit after another after another, and he couldn't help but feel like the rival contracting group, Rockwood, was at the heart of it all.

Ever since Conflux, a company they had been hired to help keep secure a few months back, had fallen under attack by Rockwood, the Shadow team had been having regular run-ins with them. Months ago, Rockwood had lost out on a major contract, to manufacture machines and parts for the US government, to Conflux. That had pit the two companies against each other in an all-out cyberwar, complete with corporate spies and counterspies.

After the STEALTH team had exposed the group for illicit dealings, they promised revenge. Now, anytime something bad happened within a hundred-mile radius of one of their contractors, AJ constantly found himself looking for the Rockwood operative who had pulled the trigger.

Even now, with the rogue bear, he couldn't help but wonder if somehow they were involved in its sudden appearance at the ranch. Sure, he understood bears came and went, but this one seemed hell-bent on keeping AJ from doing his normal job—a job that required a lot of brain space and even more concentration.

The game warden was walking around the snow-covered meadow and occasionally crouching down as she studied the area. Truth be told, she wasn't a bad-looking woman. He liked her long blond hair pulled into a ponytail at the base of her neck. He could imagine her letting it fall loose around her shoulders after she slipped out of her brown uniform.

The top two buttons of her shirt were unbuttoned, which meant she was probably not as high and tight as many of the women he knew in law enforcement—women who had had to fit in with the men around them and the only way to do that was to make themselves as asexual and untouchable as possible. Though, not all were of that way of thinking. He'd also met a few women who aimed to control the men they worked with through physical manipulation; the woman in front of him didn't seem like that kind, either.

If anything, Amber seemed like the kind of woman who just didn't notice. She lived in her own world, probably one in which she spent copious amounts of time in her truck, driving around from one fishing access to another. There were likely interesting moments in her job, and even more curious investigations into poaching and missing persons, but by and large her job seemed far simpler than his as head of the STEALTH Shadow team— he envied her that.

"Find the bear yet?" he called out the window after her, knowing full well he was being a smart-ass and was probably going to piss her off.

She glowered at him as he got out and started to walk toward her. "Yeah, it's standing right behind you."

She said something else that he couldn't quite hear, but he was sure was something to the effect that she hoped it really was…and that it was a second away from mauling him while she watched and took pictures to show her friends.

Yeah, she was definitely the highlight of all the crap that was happening. If anything, it was nice to be around someone who didn't resent him for his job and only resented him for his presence—he could work with that, maybe even make her realize he was not as big a pain in the ass as she appeared to believe. Then again, that would be a long shot. He couldn't remember the last person who didn't think of him as a pain in the ass.

"Seriously, though," he began. "The bear has been frequenting this area. I'm surprised you are having to search for bear sign."

"Oh, no," she chuckled. "I'm finding sign." She pointed in the direction of a large black pile of scat to her left. "If anything, I'm actually wondering what it has been feeding on." She turned her back to him, hunching over as she made her way deeper into the timber that stood around them like black, mossy ghosts.

He followed behind, looking deeper into the trees. The hairs on the back of his neck and down his arms prickled. God, he hated that feeling.

Running his hand over the back of his neck,

he tried to get control of himself. There was nothing and no one around; it was just his imagination getting the better of him. Just because the bear had been frequenting the area didn't mean that he hadn't just as easily decided to move along. It was just the nature of his job getting to him, making him look for threats everywhere.

His world was filled with secrets—none greater than the fact he hated being alone. If anyone looked from the outside, they would have probably assumed he was the kind who relished the freedom that came with being a single man in power. With all of his siblings shacking up and getting married, he had come to realize that work didn't have to be everything and threats didn't have to exist everywhere. But he'd become so used to the constant motion and requirements of his job, he wasn't sure how he could make time in his schedule for anything else.

"You coming?" She looked back at him, making him realize he had somehow fallen behind her thanks to his bevy of thoughts. She started to turn back, but suddenly stopped. "What in the hell?" She darted into the shadows cast by the shrouded trees.

He hurried to catch up, skirting around the skeletal branches that reached out to him like hands. One caught him across the cheek, just hard enough to sting but hopefully not deep enough to draw blood.

Running his finger over his cheek, he glanced down at his hands. There was nothing on his fingers, but on the snow below were dark speckles of blood. He grabbed for his cheek, but it wasn't wet or sticky like he had expected.

"AJ!" Amber's eyes were wide and she motioned wildly for him to come to her. "AJ, look at this." She pointed to the ground.

He carefully stepped over the blood by the tips of his boots—telling himself it was nothing—as he went to her.

There, lying next to a downed tree that had turned gray with age and weather, was a long yellowish bone. Drawing closer, he sucked in a breath. Near the ground, covered by part of the dead log, was a mass of flesh. It was stringy and loose where it must have gone through the teeth of the bear, who'd scavenged and left it looking like pieces of floss.

He didn't want to disturb the remains, but he picked up a stick and pushed back a bit of the cold, stiff flesh. Flipping it up, he found a hand. A woman's... On the middle finger of the right hand was a sapphire ring—one that he knew all too well.

He'd spent hours poring over the design and how the white gold was meant to swirl around the three sapphires, each one steadily darker and a deeper blue than the one before.

Sinking to his knees, he stared at the ring as he hoped he was wrong. Yet, there was no denying it—it was the engagement ring he'd given to his ex. It was a ring she had never returned, but instead had worn to meet her death.

Chapter Three

Death was a constant in her line of work. Amber had started to wonder if she was even some sort of grim reaper, one who carried a Glock instead of a scythe. It was an unfortunate side of her job, spent out in nature, that she regularly had to face the downside of living—dying.

It sucked, there was no other word to describe it, but at the end of the day she had to look at death as just another soul passing through this plane and moving to the next.

All of that being said, it wasn't every day that she had to face the death of a person, or at least human remains. Without a team to come in here and take inventory of the scene, it would be hard to say just how long the person, whose hand they had found, had been down. It had been cold now for a spell, which kept decomp to a minimum. Over a winter, remains could appear as fresh as if the animal had died a matter of days before.

She stared down at the partially chewed-on hand. There were tooth marks at the wrist where the bear had gnawed away at the bones and fascia. The animal had probably held down the hand like a dog chewing a bone, working it sideways in an attempt to get the high-fat and nutritious marrow. There was a bit of dirt between each of the fingers and the fingertips had turned a dark shade of purple. The nails were longer than hers, but the beds looked as though they had started to shrink with cold and time, pulling back from the nails and making them appear longer than they had when the person had been alive.

She didn't want to touch the hand or disturb the scene. They would have to call in the sheriff's office on this one. She let out an embittered laugh at the thought.

"Amber, you okay?"

She jerked as she looked up and remembered that she wasn't alone. "Yeah, sorry."

She hadn't noticed until now, but the man's face—which had been pinkened by the cold—was now lacking color. "Are you okay?"

He looked away from her, turning so she couldn't see his face. "I'm fine, but what were you laughing about?"

"I didn't mean to laugh. I'm around death a lot, and it just never gets easier."

At that, he swiped a hand over his nose and turned back. "That... That is something I *totally* understand. Death is...it's always hard to face." The way he spoke made it clear there was something to his admission—more than simply met the eye.

It made her wonder exactly who this man was. He hadn't really told her much about what he did here and what he had given her had been ambiguous.

"You around death a lot, too?" she asked, trying not to raise her eyebrows and give away her leading question. "What kind of *club* are you in, exactly?"

AJ ran his hand around the back of his neck and peered up at the sky. "We are security consultants."

That didn't really answer her question and it irked her. "Seriously? What in the hell is that supposed to mean?" She tried to stop the annoyance from entering her voice, but it was too late so she rolled with it, crossing her arms over her chest as she instinctively stuck out her hip and cocked a brow.

"Ha," he said, "I should have known that wouldn't satisfy you."

There he went, intensifying her annoyance. They'd just found a body on his property and he seemed determined to be evasive. She didn't suspect him for a minute—the look on his face moments ago said he was just as shocked as she was, but now wasn't the time to play coy with what was going on here. "Answer."

He gave her a smirk that was entirely too sexy for her liking. Especially when she was playing good cop and trying to get answers that he wasn't keen on giving. "That smile may get you a million miles with some women, but regardless of what you think, it's not going to work on me. I'm not like most women."

"And that is exactly what most women say," he countered.

That was strike three. He was outta here. She turned away from him, starting toward her running truck, not waiting for him, or for him to realize that she wasn't here to play some stupid simpering game that he could control with a cloying smile.

She didn't slow down even when she heard the crunch of his footfalls moving fast from behind, like he was jogging to catch up to her.

"Amber, wait," he called after her.

He could be as sorry as he wanted. He'd been an ass and there was nothing he could say or do to make her think anything else about him. He'd burned their amicable bridge. Now he was a pain in her ass, nothing more…even if she had thought he was kind of cute, in a bad-boy way.

Don't give him an inch.

"Amber…" He said her name again, this time with a softness that nearly made her stop.

Instead, she slowed down and let him catch up to her side. "What?"

"I'm sorry. I'm an ass."

He could say that again. "I didn't mean to say that. I'm not that kind of guy."

"Now, that is what every guy who is *that kind of guy* says," she said, knowing it was against her better judgment to lower herself to his level, but at the same time unable to find the restraint to stop herself.

He stepped in front of her and when she looked up at him, and into his blue eyes, her breath caught in her throat and for a moment she almost forgot how to breathe. How could someone who made her so—so *pissed* one second, make her swoon the next?

Yep, I need to get away from this man as fast as humanly possible.

"Amber, I didn't mean to be an ass—it's just that all of this—" he waved in the direction of the remains "—is more than I expected."

She took a much-needed breath. "All I was asking was that you tell me a little more about yourself. You wanted to be vague."

He raised his hands, like the action was some kind of gesture of peace, but she noted that he was missing half of the middle finger on his left hand. She tried not to stare at the nub, but found her gaze drawn to the missing digit.

"It's okay, you can look at it. It got shot off during a mission." He gave her a sad smile.

She reached over and pushed down his hands. "I don't need to look at your finger."

"You want to know what a security consultant does?" He paused. "We sacrifice our bodies and souls to whomever is the highest bidder. Usually, we are on the good guy's side. Yet, even when we are fighting for what we see as justifiable reasons, we find ourselves having to make some hard choices. Choices that no one should ever have to make."

A sickening knot formed in her stomach. "If that is the kind of life you've led, why—" she motioned in the direction of the lone hand they'd found in the woods "—why would you have any problem when it came to that kind of thing? You made it sound like you didn't care about death, but your face... It said something different."

"I don't know what you mean, but that hand back there... We will deal with it. Right now, I want you to know that I am genuinely sorry for being a jerk. I had no right to treat you like I did. I know you have a job to do, but when regular people start asking questions, I get a little on-edge."

Did he mean that when people started asking questions, his life was on the line?

Given the brief amount of time she had interacted with this man, she couldn't imagine she was reading him right, but at the same time there was no denying the inflection of his words or the way his features seemed to harden when he wanted to close her out. Just now, she could see the flicker of the muscle at the edge of his jaw.

This once, she would cut him a break.

Chapter Four

AJ didn't know why he didn't tell her that he recognized the ring.

Hell, just because it looked like the one he had specially designed, it didn't mean that it was actually unique. Even if it was, it didn't mean that his ex-fiancée, Tammy, hadn't pawned it off after they had broken up. He damn well would have after their tough breakup.

He flipped up the neck of his jacket as he stood in the cold, waiting for the sheriff's deputy to arrive. It had been at least forty-five minutes since Amber had called them. Over the last few years, his family had required officer assistance on the ranch; unfortunately, he had grown used to waiting for them.

But with this incident cutting so close to him, the forty-five minutes felt more like forty-five hours.

He was tempted to walk over to where they

found the hand, but he resisted the urge. Part of him wanted to take a picture of it, and look more closely at the ring just to negate any possibility that it was actually the one he thought it was. Yet, he didn't want to draw any scrutiny if, in fact, it did turn out to be the ring he had purchased. If it was, this hand had to belong to Tammy. His stomach turned to knots.

It couldn't be her...

Amber sighed, glancing down at her watch.

"If you have somewhere to be, you don't have to wait around here with me," he said. "I'm sure that whether you are here to escort law enforcement to the hand or not, the result will be the same." As soon as he was done speaking, he wished he hadn't opened his mouth. "I mean, don't get me wrong, but I bet you have better things to do then sit around here."

He wasn't sure he had made the situation any better, especially thanks to the sour look on her face.

"Yeah, I'm not going anywhere." She leaned up against her truck, crossing her arms over her chest.

He had seen her do that a couple of times now when talking to him. It made him wonder if there was any chance whatsoever of them moving past antagonizing one another. He really needed a friend right now, and there was something about her that wasn't too bad. If they just met at a bar, or at some kind of social gathering, he probably would have even thought she was datable.

He'd much rather take things slow with women, get to know them and love them for who they were rather than just jumping straight into bed. Sex was easy, but having a real relationship that meant something was damn near impossible.

Relationships, whether they were friendship or romantic, took far more effort than any facet of his job as the leader for STEALTH Shadow team. Just the relationships with his siblings took more out of him than he wanted to give, but for them he would make exceptions. They drove him nuts, but they were his people, his *tribe*. Regardless of what the world threw at them, they would always be a single unit. That, in and of itself, was worth whatever emotional turmoil it created.

Relationships built around sex didn't last. He'd learned his lesson when it came to that one, thanks to Tammy. They'd had incredible passion, but when they weren't having sex, they were fighting and things eventually fizzled out. Unfortunately, once again, she had found her way back into his life. Even if that hand wasn't hers, it was like she was a ghost who was constantly haunting him. He would never be free of her.

"You know, *you* don't have to stick around." Amber looked at him as she spoke.

There was something about the darkness in her eyes, or maybe it was the tone of her voice, but he wanted to take her hands in his and tell her it was all going to be okay.

What is wrong with me? He felt like a hot-mess dumpster fire, out of control of his emotions… especially when it came to women.

Maybe it was best if he did leave. He could call Zoey Martin, head of STEALTH, and have her come out and deal with all this, but if he did, he was sure he would hear about it. She had a million commitments—which was exactly why she had hired him and his family as a secondary team and why he needed to be the leader she expected. He pulled out his phone and sent a quick text to her, letting her know what they had found on the ranch. She couldn't be kept in the dark about this, or she would be pissed.

"You don't think the bear is going to come back tonight, do you?" he asked, sidestepping Amber having basically asked him to leave.

"There is only another hour or two of daylight. If the bear is going to come back, I bet it will be closer to dusk. They are diurnal, but they do most of their moving around at night in order to avoid people. That being said, you mentioned that you have seen this bear during the day?" she asked.

He nodded. "Yeah, my sister told me she had seen it by our barn a few days ago. We have a lot of deer, whitetails mostly, up by the house. It was early morning—the bear may have been taking a look for easy prey before moving to the woods to sleep for the day." He shrugged.

"You're probably right. They don't like a lot of activity. More solitary creatures." She dropped her arms to her sides. "By the way, how many siblings do you have?"

Finally, he was getting somewhere with her. Inch by inch, maybe they would become friends, but only time would tell. "I'm one of six kids. Our parents passed away a few years ago in a car accident and we took over the family business before it was bought and moved under the STEALTH umbrella."

He wasn't sure why he had said that, but a softness returned to her features, and he was glad he had opened up.

"Do all of your siblings live here on the ranch?" She seemed genuinely interested.

"Most of them do. Every one of my siblings works for the team, though. Recently, my sister Kendra moved back to Montana to be with her fiancé. She's an attorney and he's a bounty hunter—interesting stuff."

She looked a bit surprised. "So all of your family members are badasses?" She smiled, and as she did, there was the sparkle in her eyes that made them appear even bluer than before.

Yeah, a man could definitely be moved by a smile and a look like that. She was beautiful.

"Yeah, everybody but me." He sent her a half smile, but it was weighed down with his concern for Tammy. "I'm just an average dude, with a badass job." He forced a chuckle. "But come on now, you're pretty interesting yourself. You have to admit not everyone spends their days worrying about being attacked by a grizzly bear."

"We are not going to be attacked by a grizzly bear," she said with a chuff, like such an idea was unfathomable, even though there was evidence that the bear had made lunch of another person.

"True, *you* are probably more likely to attack," he teased.

She sent him a quelling look.

"Ouch," he said.

Her cheeks darkened with a blush.

He grinned. He couldn't help but enjoy the

way that blush brightened her cheeks and made her look more delicate. "It's fine. I'm teasing you. I'm just glad you decided you can finally like me."

She pulled back, giving him an appraising look. "Who said I liked you?" There was a playful edge to her voice.

"There are only two reasons for you to use your verbal claws on me. One, I'm a jerk and I deserve it. Which, I guess, could be the case." He laughed. "Or, what I assume is going on here, maybe you kind of like me." He wasn't sure why he'd said it, and unease swept through him. Considering what had forced them together in this situation, the last thing he should be doing was flirting. But he couldn't help it. It had been a hellish day and she was distracting him.

She looked totally affronted by the idea and the accusation, and she opened her mouth to speak but before she could, there was the crunch of gravel in the distance, and they looked over to see a four-wheeler careening toward them.

Son of a...

The vehicle came to a skidding stop behind the warden's pickup, and a woman stepped off and slipped the helmet from her head. Zoey Martin's black-and-blue hair was longer than it normally was and she had a large ring in her nose today.

She looked from Amber to him, seeming to sense the awkwardness between them, and smirked. "What in the hell is happening out here?"

"Nice to see you, too," he said. "Zoey, this is Amber Daniels, the game warden we called to get this bear situation under control."

"Charmed," Zoey clipped. "So how exactly does a game warden and my employee come up with a hand when they are out looking for a bear?"

Amber shot him a look, like she was disappointed in him for having let the cat out of the bag.

Zoey walked past them, in the direction of their footprints in the snow. "Where is this hand?"

"Out there, at your three o'clock," he said, motioning her ahead. He waited with Amber for a moment, until Zoey was out of earshot. "Hey," he whispered, "I'm sorry about her. She has zero tact. Her world is blood and war. Be patient with her."

Amber opened and closed her mouth, but instead of saying anything, she simply nodded. She followed Zoey, unsteady as she stepped into the uneven and crunching snow.

He had finally started to gain ground with Amber, and now he was losing it all over again.

Hell, maybe it was a good thing.

After being with Tammy, who had hated him so much, he shouldn't be thinking about getting involved with any woman.

Just as he started to follow Amber, there was the sound of another car approaching. He turned as a deputy pulled up in a Chevy Tahoe. They hadn't been running lights, and he was glad. They didn't need to draw scrutiny from their neighbors or passersby. Sure, they were a ways from the road and public areas, but that didn't mean crap out here.

Zoey whistled at them. "Tell him to meet us over here," she called, sounding annoyed at the dog and pony show that this was already starting to become.

"You got it, boss." He didn't normally call her "boss," but it felt right with Amber there with them.

Yeah, he needed to get over his need to posture for that woman.

The deputy turned on his interior light and he could see the dark-haired guy talking on his handset. No doubt, he was letting Dispatch know his location and his objective. That was how he ran his team, and police were much like the Shadow team.

AJ slowly made his way over to the guy's rig and waited for him to get off his radio and open his door. The deputy stepped out and AJ recognized him as Deputy Terrell, a guy he had spoken to, though infrequently, when he'd been to the ranch in the past. "How's it going, Terrell?" he asked, making sure to give his voice as friendly an air as possible.

"Things are going all right. Can't complain." The man stepped out and put his hands in his utility belt, instinctively framing his junk like it was some primal display of dominance.

"Well, we certainly appreciate you coming here and helping us out. Just sorry it has to be under these kinds of conditions. Ya know?" He tried to throw the guy a proverbial win in the game AJ didn't want to play.

The deputy nodded. "I read you all found what you think are human remains out here? You got any idea how they got here?" The guy moved his hands up and latched his thumbs under the edges of his bulletproof vest.

"We called in the game warden—Amber," AJ said, motioning in her direction, "to help us with a rogue griz we have on the property. It's been roaming around looking for food. Looks like it was down here munching on a body."

The deputy drew back slightly. "Oh, damn. Bear and a body. You definitely got your hands full with all the things happening out here at the ranch. You guys are always busy."

Damn it. The guy definitely had a long memory and that wouldn't do them any favors when it came to these remains and the investigation that would likely ensue—his family definitely had a reputation when it came to causing upheaval in the community.

"We do try to keep things to a low roar, but you can't control everything on a place like this. Just too much land to cover and people to keep track of," he said, though he didn't mean any of it. "The hand is over there. Zoey wanted to take a peek before you arrived."

He turned from the deputy and started leading him over to the remains. He didn't really want to be a part of this investigation, but if he was going to be in for a penny, he was going to be in for a pound. Whether he liked it or not, he had been on scene when the hand had been located.

The deputy started toward Zoey and Amber. "Hey, you guys, you want to take a step back from there? Let's try not to contaminate our scene any more than necessary."

Amber nodded and waited for Zoey as she turned away from the hand in the snow. Zoey looked straight at AJ and glared. Had she recognized the ring?

No.

There was no way Zoey would know that ring or whom it had belonged to. He hadn't been engaged to Tammy at the time his family's company had moved under STEALTH. That had happened later. Then again, Zoey was the queen of information gathering. That woman knew everything and didn't let a damn thing slide. No doubt, she had done her due diligence and done all kinds of digging into each and every one of the Spade siblings' lives. She wasn't one to miss things.

But he wasn't about to say anything to her out here, or in front of law enforcement. His best defense now would be a strong offense, regardless of the fact that he had done nothing wrong. But when it came to the murder of a woman, it was definitely the love interest or former love interest that was the first one to go on the suspects list. Not to mention the fact that, if this was Tammy, her remains were now on their ranch.

He was so screwed. If he was lead detective on this investigation, it would take him ten hours max to get a positive identification on the remains. From there, it would only be a few more hours before the police would be looking right at him.

It was crazy how fast a person could get tracked down in the electronic age.

He could very well be arrested before the end of tomorrow.

Yeah, there was no way he could allow that to happen. He needed time to find out if these really were Tammy's remains, and if they were, he needed to come up with one hell of an alibi in order to clear his name.

As much as he wanted to keep on the right side of law enforcement, he had to buy himself more time before they started poking around the ranch and collecting evidence. At the very least, he needed to talk to his sister Kendra, who was also the family attorney. She would have all the answers and tell him exactly what he needed to do.

"Hey, Terrell?" he called after the deputy, who turned and faced him.

"What's up?" Terrell asked, almost side by side with Zoey and Amber.

"I'm sure that Zoey, the owner of the ranch, will be on board with me on this. Our lawyer can get a bit salty when not kept in the loop when it comes to law enforcement getting involved with our family's business," he said, giving Zoey a pointed look. "As such, I think it would be best if we put a pin in this for a bit. I'm going to need you to get a search warrant before you take one more step toward those remains."

Zoey frowned, but then her face went blank. Amber looked shocked. "AJ…"

"I'm sorry, but I think until we talk to our attorney and get things cleared from a business level on our side, it is best if you both, Amber and Terrell, don't do anything more until you get a warrant."

Amber turned away and started to walk to her truck, not looking back at him as she strode away.

He tried to ignore the ache in his chest, but just like that, there was no doubt that any chance he had with Amber had just gone out the window.

Chapter Five

Amber shouldn't have been hurt, but she couldn't help the way she felt when it came to AJ. He was everything she both loved and hated when it came to men. He was the embodiment of desire and lust, secrets and truth, loneliness and company. And damn if he wasn't the sexiest man she'd ever met.

Not that she could officially say that he was sexy—that would be unprofessional and stupid. Sure, she had made a lot of stupid decisions in the past when it came to dating the wrong men, but that was when she had been young and dumb...and she'd made sure to keep them out of her parents' line of sight. When she turned thirty, she'd promised herself that those days were behind her; and if a man came into her life, their relationship was going to be healthy from the very beginning or it wasn't going to happen.

She didn't have the time or the patience to

deal with any kind of toxic behavior in her private life. Especially when the toxicity came in the form of a man whom she had no business desiring, and who had literally kicked her off her investigation an hour before.

Yes, she definitely didn't like him. Not even a little bit.

Everything about him screamed that she should run, and yet here she stood on the road at the center of the ranch, waiting on a search warrant with the police officer so she could remain near him. Well, not *him* exactly.

"I appreciate you sticking around," Deputy Terrell said, breaking the silence as he stood beside his car, a spotting scope aimed at the area so they could make sure the scene was in no way being tampered with while they waited for the warrant. "I would like to get the trap sorted out for the bear. Last thing my team needs, while they are poring through this, is to run headlong into a hungry bear."

"Yeah. It's no problem." The sun was starting to set and if she'd had her way, she would have already had the trap dropped and baited. "With food sources around, that bear isn't going to go too far. Once you get the warrant, I'll just get the trap set and I'll get out of your hair."

Terrell frowned. "Actually, we have a lot of

officers out right now, and I could use an extra hand securing the scene. I mean, if you're not too busy."

As a game warden, she was a sworn officer with statewide law-enforcement authority. But she knew how police officers saw them—most of the time they simply assumed that game wardens were people who couldn't make the cut, or couldn't deal with the politics of working in their police department. That wasn't the case for her. She had no desire to be a deputy, but she did enjoy helping them out. Knowing how he would perceive her, however, she had to play it cool and not sound too eager.

"Yeah, it's been a long day, but I have no problem sticking around for a few more hours if you need me. I know how it is working with a skeleton crew. We only have sixteen game wardens in the entire state of Montana. We're running at half staff."

"It shouldn't be too much longer to get on the scene. The detective on this has already heard back from the county attorney, so all I need now is the approval from the judge. We'll be back on this investigation in no time, and from there we'll just be waiting for the detective to arrive."

Zoey and AJ had disappeared back to the main house, no doubt coming up with a game plan of how to handle the situation. She didn't envy them for having to go through this. By now they were probably regretting their decision in having a game warden show up at the ranch at all.

If Zoey was the kind of woman Amber thought she was, she was probably chewing AJ's ass right now and telling him a thousand things he should have done instead of calling her in. Though Amber shouldn't have felt bad for bringing this drama to their doorstep, she did. In no way was this her doing, but she still felt responsible for all of the complications that were about to rain down.

She hated that she had all these feelings. This was work, he was work, and this was all nothing more. To treat it as anything other than that was just setting herself up for hurt and failure, neither of which she enjoyed. Besides, it wasn't like he was even that great, anyway. AJ had been nothing but a pain in her ass since the moment she'd arrived here. Why call in the police and then send them away? What had changed?

The deputy's phone pinged. "Looks like we got it. Detective Baker is asking that we give them five minutes before we go down and completely rope off the scene."

"Why would he ask for something like that? Doesn't he want us to get started?"

Terrell looked at her like she had lost her mind. "Do you have any clue who this family is? Who they run with? Or what they do?"

The way he asked the questions made her wonder if she was the last person in the entire state to understand who AJ Spade and his family were, and then she thought about the conversation she'd had with AJ earlier. He made it sound like they were not a family that was well-known in the area, nor did they wish to be, and yet, it seemed as though they had one hell of a reputation—one that had inspired the police to give them some sort of professional courtesy.

"No," she said, pinching her lips and shaking her head. "Is there something I need to know before I head back out there? I don't want to walk into the line of fire without a clue."

"So the company your buddy there works for…" He nudged his chin in the direction of the ranch house. She wanted to tell him that in no way was AJ her friend, but she held off. "They are a world leader in private military contracting. When you think of black ops and assassins, those are the guys."

Her stomach dropped. Of course, she would be attracted to the most dangerous dude possible. Why couldn't she just be attracted to an accountant type her parents would adore? They would love nothing more than to see her happy and with a safe man, especially after all the grief their family had gone through.

"Well, I guess I know why you didn't want me to leave you out here alone." She audibly groaned. "All that being said, I don't quite understand why the detective would want us to wait."

"Detective Baker is a good dude, and he has worked with this family in the past. I don't know all the ins and outs, but they definitely have adequate respect for one another."

"But waiting to investigate an unwitnessed death…"

There came that look again from Terrell. "The remains being out here is odd and probably not just random. Yet, they may not have anything to do with them. I've come to learn that this family is on a lot of people's hit lists. And I'm not just talking about single individuals, but entire countries who want them dead."

A knot formed in her stomach. Just who were the Spades? There were definitely people who didn't like her for the job she was hired to do, but she had never gotten an impression that any wished her dead. She couldn't even begin to imagine how that must have affected

AJ and his team. The only things that had ever really wanted Amber dead had been a protective cow moose with her calf, and the bear who had taken a swipe.

The door to the ranch house opened and at least ten people came walking out. No one appeared to be armed, but if she had to guess, thanks to the no-nonsense looks on their faces, they were all carrying.

Suddenly, this was starting to feel all too much like the Old-West shoot-out at the O.K. Corral. One false move and guns would be blazing. Few, if any, would be left standing.

If things went in that direction, she doubted she and Terrell would make it off this ranch.

A cold chill moved down her spine. This was what she got for wanting to stop a grizzly from getting killed.

Last to come out of the door were Zoey and AJ. It surprised her, but AJ looked calm. Maybe she had gotten it all wrong in assuming that Zoey would be upset with him. Or maybe this was all just an act in order to make her and Terrell feel completely out of their element. If that was the case, they didn't need to try so hard.

From behind her, she could hear car tires crunching on the gravel as a vehicle made its way toward them. Hopefully it was the detective, and he'd come with backup.

A black Suburban pulled to a stop next to Terrell's car. Stepping out was a stout man, with frosted tips on his dark hair. He had a serious look on his face and he said something to the deputy she couldn't quite hear.

Zoey Martin made her way out toward their caravan, like she was coming to parley. Everything about this felt like a battle, but Amber couldn't quite pinpoint why. This family had nothing to hide, and AJ had nothing to hide… right? There was no reason for a standoff.

"Detective Baker, how the hell are you?" Zoey said once she'd approached, throwing her arms up jovially in the air. Her hair blew slightly in the wind as she came over and wrapped her arms around the detective.

Detective Baker was all smiles as he looked at her. "What in the hell is up with this needing-a-search-warrant crap?" Detective Baker leaned back from their embrace and took her by the shoulders. "I was just sitting down for dinner. If you needed something, you should have just called. This is ridiculous."

Zoey looked to Amber and the deputy before glancing back to Baker. "You know as well as I do that sometimes we have to dot the i's and cross the t's, and you know…all the things." She stepped out of Baker's grip. "With so much going on, we just have to make sure that we make our lawyers happy. You know how it is." She chuckled, but as far as Amber was concerned there was nothing funny about the situation.

Ninety seconds ago, everyone had seemed ready to draw down and shoot anyone who got in their line of sight.

"Damn, don't I know how you feel. Lawyers are nothing but a pain in the ass." Baker reached behind his back and pulled out a set of papers, then handed them over to Zoey. "Here, these are for your lawyers, and I'm sure for mine as well."

"Much appreciated," Zoey said, taking the papers and putting them in her back pocket without even looking. "Now, let's get your team back there and get things going. We really have no intention of making this investigation any harder than necessary. We want to get to the bottom of this just as much as you do."

Detective Baker gave her a pointed look that made Amber wonder what they had just exchanged nonverbally.

Amber's gaze moved to AJ, and she found that he was staring at her. For a second, their eyes locked and then he quickly glanced away. What was it about this family that they wanted to only communicate with glances and they couldn't just talk like normal people?

But, of course, assassins wouldn't be that kind.

Assassins. The word rattled through her.

This morning, a team of black-ops assassins would have been the last thing she would've thought she would be dealing with. If asked, she wasn't sure she would have wanted to take this call again. AJ was a beautiful man with a dangerous job, which was one hell of a good reason to stay as far away as possible.

Suddenly, she missed driving aimlessly around in her pickup truck looking for illegal operations in the woods. She would take a team of hillbillies any day over a family of black-ops members and their bosses. Before this thing with him went any further and she got any more confused, she needed to handle her business with Terrell and the bear, and then get off this ranch.

She moved toward the others, but AJ came toward her with a smile. "I was thinking I'd come help you set that bear trap. We still need to get that situation under control."

Before she even realized what she was doing, she jerked away from him. Though she wasn't sure if she was right or not, she had a feeling that she was safer with the bear.

Confusion swept across his face at her sudden reaction.

But that smile he'd given a moment before… She didn't trust that, either. What was he playing at? "What is going on with you?" She studied him for a long moment, watching as his smile faded.

"Huh? What do you mean?" He motioned for her to walk with him toward her truck.

"The last time I spoke to you, you were telling us to leave."

"Yes, but did you leave?" He gave her a side look as he walked to the driver's door and opened it up for her. "No, you didn't," he responded for her. "Just as I knew you wouldn't."

"I could have left," she countered, getting into the pickup and turning on the engine while she waited for him to get in on the passenger side.

"You could have, but that's not like you," he said as he got in.

She turned to him and put up her hand, stopping him. "You know, you seem to have a constant issue with assuming you know more about me than you do. You have no idea who I am."

He gave her a cute, albeit somewhat dismissive, smile. "Amber Daniels. You're thirty years old. No children. You've never been married. You have a bachelor's degree in wildlife biology from MSU. Your favorite color is green. Your eyes are blue. And your parents think you're perfect. You never give them any problems."

"Wait… What the hell? You talked to my parents?" She dropped her hands onto the steering wheel. The rest of the people AJ had come out with were getting into trucks and following the detective and the deputy as they made their way down the road and toward the remains.

She wasn't going to put this truck in Drive until she was sure she wanted him at her side. This man, this infuriating, terrifying and impressive man, was constantly throwing her for a loop. She didn't like it.

"Strictly speaking, I never spoke with your parents, but my brother Mike did." He pointed at the stocky man with dark hair in the passenger side of the nearest pickup. "I gotta say, what we managed to pull about you in just a matter of hours was impressive. You've done a lot of good things in your time as sergeant." He motioned after the taillights that were starting to disappear into the darkness as Mike and the rest of his team made their way into the encroaching darkness. "We should probably catch up."

Right now, the only place she was tempted to take this truck was anywhere that didn't involve this invasive family. "I don't know who you think you are, but you and your team shouldn't be contacting my parents without my consent or knowledge."

As she thought about her mom, who was in her early seventies, she got instantly furious. The last thing her parents needed was some nosy jerk calling them and making them worry about her. They had more than enough going on in their lives that they didn't need to fuss over Amber's welfare.

This guy knew every button to push when it came to making her angry.

"I can see this is upsetting for you, but that wasn't my intention. It really was meant to be a compliment," he added. "There're very few people who are actually *good* in this world, and I have to say I think you are one of them."

"Clearly, you are *not* one of the good ones," she countered, anger marring her tone.

He chuckled, as if he was enjoying her frustration. "You are going to regret saying that to me later, you and I both know. So in an effort to save you an apology... It's accepted already and we can move on from this." He grinned at her. "Besides, I'm sure that by now you did a little digging and you know exactly who I am and what our team does. I'm proud of the work that we do, by the way."

She wanted to bite at him again, but he was probably right about feeling bad, and she would regret going for the jugular. "How did you know I wouldn't leave? And why do you feel the need to dig into me? Between the two of us…"

His smile widened and she felt the gravitational pull of it, so she put the truck in gear and started down the dirt road after the rest of the convoy.

"I like to know who I'm working with. I've learned the hard way that sometimes it's the ones we care for who have the power to hurt us the most."

It was quiet as they drove to where everyone had parked. She wanted to dislike him, but couldn't find a real reason when he had been so complimentary of her. On the other hand, she was going to need to talk to her parents about not giving strangers personal information about their family. At least it sounded like they had avoided the topic of her brother.

"Hey," AJ said, "for what it's worth, I'm sorry about shutting you guys down. I admit I got a little freaked out with the hand and stuff. A lot of people depend on me to make good choices, and sometimes it can be overwhelming. My asking you to stop wasn't personal."

Before she had a chance to respond, he jumped out of the pickup and started after his teams.

With him went her chances of trying to dislike him.

Assassin or not, he was a good guy with a lot on his plate. There were definitely things going on in his life that she didn't understand, nor would she probably ever understand, but she could tell he was doing the best he could.

His opening up to her had to be hard for him and yet he was still talking. It said so much about how he felt about her; and against her better judgment, she was flattered he had chosen to open up. She doubted he spoke to many people with the level of honesty that he had just bestowed upon her.

She walked out into the meadow. Before everything had gone haywire, she had found a location that would have made a perfect spot for her to drop the trap. However, she would need to move away from the location a bit, so if they were working around the area, she wouldn't draw a bear. They didn't like a lot of activity, but the bait had the potential to override their fear. They didn't need an investigator having a run-in with a hungry griz.

She walked over to the working team and approached AJ. "I'm going to drop the trap." She motioned to the back of her pickup where the trap sat. "I'll put it down a couple draws over, check in with Terrell and then head out."

"You mind if I help you?" he asked, surprising her.

She nodded and they walked back to the pickup. She made her way down the road until she couldn't see the officers or their cars anymore. She found a spot up a ravine between two large pines and a new growth stand that would act as a natural corral and push the bear into the trap instead of going around. It would work well if the bear wasn't savvy. If it had been caught before, or tagged, it would be another story.

They didn't talk and AJ just went to work as if he had done this kind of thing before. He waved her back as she reversed into position to lower the trap.

It only took a few minutes to release the winch and let the culvert trap drop into place. She had thrown in a roadkill carcass, and after opening the trap, she made her way inside and quickly hung it up. It had been dead for a while and the smell, even in the cold, was something she was wondering if she would be able to get out of her hair in one wash. Bears were notorious scavengers and often took on the fetid odor of the carrion in which they had been feasting. There was little doubt that it was the scent of the remains that had likely brought the bear to the property. Although, bears were also known for killing the weak.

Had that been the victim—the weak?

Coming out of the trap, she glanced back at her handiwork as she took off her work gloves and slapped them against her leg. AJ stood beside her. "Good work, warden."

She smiled. "This isn't my first rodeo."

"I can tell," he said as they got back into the pickup and rolled toward the squad. "I don't even know why you let me help you. It was clear you didn't need me. You just rolled right in and started dropping it down without an issue."

"I wanted you to think you were being helpful." She inadvertently fluttered her eyelashes as she smiled. *What in the hell? I have stink on my hands and I'm flirting?*

AJ laughed, his breath coming out as a long cloud. "Yes, I definitely need to feel helpful. It's what keeps me going."

She smiled, soaking up his laughter. He really was a sexy man. It was just unfortunate that this would likely be the last time she would see him.

She stopped behind what was steadily turning into a parking lot in the woods. "Speaking of going—" she nudged her chin in the direction of law enforcement and his team "—I'm going to get outta here. It's a long ride home and I have to work tomorrow so I guess this is goodbye." She tried to keep the sadness out of her voice, but she could hear it fleck her tone. Hopefully, he couldn't hear it.

"You're from Superior, right?" AJ asked, opening the passenger door of the pickup and stepping out.

She was sure he had probably already memorized her address as well. As much as she should have been annoyed, she did find it a little endearing. "Yep, it's about a two-and-a-half-hour drive from here. If I hurry home, I will get maybe five hours of sleep before I have to be back at it in the morning." She took another look in the direction of the trap. "As far as this trap goes, I would recommend that no one comes near this area. Let the bear come to us. If you see that the bear has been captured, don't be afraid to give me a call." She started to reach for her card. "Wait, you don't need my number, do you?"

"You are correct." He laughed. "Which number would you like me to call you on, your business or private line?"

AJ probably even knew her shoe size. "Either is fine."

He closed the door to her pickup.

She didn't want to say goodbye. For a moment, she didn't move. She wasn't sure why. There was nothing more she needed to do here, yet something made her want to stay.

"Hey, wait," AJ said, knocking on the window of her pickup.

She rolled down her window. "Yeah?" A police car passed by her on the small dirt road. "It looks like you guys are going to have a long night."

AJ nodded. "Yeah, but Detective Baker just asked that everyone from my team go back to the house and leave them so they could work."

"Even Zoey?" she asked, surprised.

"He did ask Zoey to leave, but I'm sure you can imagine how well that went. She will play nice, but there is zero chance that she is going to miss out on this kind of thing on her property." He paused. "As it is, do you mind giving me a ride back to the house? I'd appreciate it."

She could have been reading the situation wrong, but she had a feeling he didn't want to say goodbye, either. Or maybe, it was just that he really did want a ride back to the house and it had nothing to do with the words that would or wouldn't be said.

"Sure, hop in." She tried to cover her smile as he smacked the window and then jogged around to his side of the truck.

He got in and slammed the truck door behind himself, then sent a text before throwing his phone on the dashboard and turning to her. "Where are you supposed to be in the morning?"

"As the sergeant, I don't necessarily have to be anywhere, but I need to be rolling in on the clock by six a.m. to get my hours in. Plus, I think it's a good example for my team if I'm up and rolling when they arrive on the clock."

"But it's not you going to an office?"

She shook her head. "I just clock in on my laptop and then send off reports of my activities for the day to my lieutenant—he can be a bit of a ballbuster." She tapped on the computer between them. In many ways, her vehicle was just like any law-enforcement vehicle in its setup. She even ran red-and-blues.

"If that's the case, I don't think you should leave the ranch tonight." His arm twitched as though he was thinking about reaching over and taking her hand, but she didn't move, and he didn't, either.

As much as she wanted to take him up on it—skipping the long commute tonight and tomorrow morning was tempting—it wasn't a good idea. She shook her head.

"Before you say no, hear me out. If I hadn't requested the search warrant, you would've set that trap and been on your way hours ago rather than been held up at the ranch all day. I'm just being reasonable. I mean, it doesn't make sense to drive that far and then have to come back in the morning or whatever." He seemed to be stumbling on his words. Like he wasn't used to apologizing and making it up to people.

The thought that he was making an exception for her made some of her reticence in liking him disappear.

She chewed on her bottom lip at the thought of staying at his home overnight. Her body clenched with want.

"What do you think?" he continued, pulling her out of her thoughts. "We have plenty of extra cabins. You can have one completely to yourself." He pointed in the direction of a set of row houses that ran behind the main ranch house and to the west of the barn. "There is one that has a huge rain showerhead."

"Where do you live?" she asked, trying her best not to think about him taking a shower with her in their private cabin.

"I live in one of the row houses. There are a

few private cabins on the edges of the ranch's property, too. They aren't as nice, though…"

Despite her mind telling her to stay away from AJ, she could feel the weariness of the long day slip through her. The promise of sleep was too appealing. "I… Yeah. If you don't mind… Sure."

His smile widened, causing her body to suddenly wake up. "Turn here."

Suddenly too aware of the small space they shared in the cab, her hands threatened to shake if she let go of the steering wheel as she followed his directions and stopped at the house second from the end. It was a log cabin, with a green galvanized steel roof and cute green shutters. It looked as though it had been recently built, the logs still the beautiful rich tawny browns of fresh oil, not the gray that crept in with hours of drying sun.

It was a cute place, a far cry from her 1914 cottage house, complete with knob and tube wiring and a leaking toilet that refilled every thirty minutes or so. Sadly, the sound of water running was one of the few comforts in her place. The rest of the night was filled with the sound of wind against the thin glass of the windows, and various creaks and rattles as the ground settled beneath the foundation.

She parked and he moved to get out. "I'm just

two doors down. If you need anything, whatever it is—ice, beer... Whatever. I'm here."

Just like that, any desire to actually get some sleep and then catch the bear drifted from her mind. Every thought was quickly replaced by those of AJ, and exactly how he would feel between her thighs.

Chapter Six

He didn't often find he needed to drink, but tonight was one of those rare nights. After grabbing a beer from his fridge and flipping the lid into the trash, he walked out to the back porch of his cabin. His hair was still damp from his shower, but the air felt good on his skin. It was a cold night, but he wasn't sure if he wanted to get a campfire going or just go back inside.

He took a long drink of his beer and stared out at the cloudless night. There was a crescent moon and from where he stood, he could make out the riverlike Milky Way. To the north, there were wisps of reds and greens as the aurora borealis danced in the sky.

The lights were on in Amber's cabin, and he was tempted to go over and knock on her door and make her come outside to see the ballet of colors, but he stopped himself. Though he wanted nothing more than to show her nature's beauty, he couldn't. She wasn't going to stick around here for any real amount of time. He was already far too attracted to her for his own liking. Besides, he needed to get answers about the hand and Tammy.

If he had been smarter, he would have found another place to stay tonight—somewhere that wouldn't have been a quick walk to her bedroom. He only had so much willpower.

He could see Amber walk into the bedroom and move toward the bed. She pulled the Velcro from her Kevlar vest. Though he knew he should look away, he watched as she lifted it over her head.

There had been no doubt she was beautiful and had a great body before she had taken off her vest, but now, seeing her with just her uniform on…she was breathtaking. Her ass was in perfect proportion to her breasts and he wasn't sure, if he had been in the room with her, which he would have wanted to put his hands on first. She reached down and unbuttoned her brown shirt.

His mouth watered as he turned his back to her window and tried to stare at the northern lights. As majestic as they were, they didn't have the same pull as the beauty of nature behind him.

Before he had a chance to take a second drink from his beer, his phone pinged. It was a message from Zoey. The words were simple, but he hated everything that they implied: We need to talk.

That message never meant anything good. The last time he had gotten that exact text was from Tammy. What followed was her breaking off the engagement. He liked to tell himself that the only triggers he had were on his guns, but reading that text message, he knew that wasn't true. Or maybe, it was just the day and everything that had happened that was making him more sensitive than usual.

What's up? he texted back.

In true Zoey style, she answered instantly. My office. 5 mins.

She was never one to mince words.

He made his way back inside, taking one more glance in Amber's direction, but her lights had been turned off. At the very least, he wasn't going to have to worry about his willpower anymore.

By the time he was walking into Zoey's office at the far end of the main house, his stomach had started to turn sour. It hadn't been a long walk, but it felt like his legs were made of lead as he stopped at the door and knocked.

He could only imagine the number of things that she would want to chew him out for now. Zoey had definitely gone to town on him about the hand and having to call in his sister Kendra, the family attorney, while they waited for the warrant. Kendra would have lost her mind if he hadn't paused everything to get her input. They didn't need any kind of additional legal issues, and hopefully by putting a pin in the recovery of the remains and the required investigation that would ensue, he and Kendra could head off any potential problems. Plus, it would give him time to come to terms with possibly losing Tammy. She had been such a big part of his life and if these remains did belong to her, he would want answers. Had she been mauled by a bear, or murdered and dumped on the ranch?

No matter how she had died, though, this couldn't all just be about him—he had his family, and their jobs and futures, to consider.

He had already screwed up. He hadn't mentioned the possibility of the ring being Tammy's or anything else. He should have, but the more and more he thought about the hand and the ring, the less likely it was that it was hers.

Even if it was, there were no documents pointing to it having come from him. He had been careful to keep his private life private, even when it came to engagements and purchases.

He loved to live in a world of cash. Someone

would really have to do some legwork when it came to connecting the ring back to him. Though, if it was Tammy's hand...

There was nothing good that would come from him swirling the drain on this. He hadn't done anything wrong. Besides, the detective was a friend of the family. That would go a long way in clearing his name of any possible suspicion...or so he hoped.

The door opened. Zoey frowned at him. "Come on." She motioned for him to come inside.

He did as ordered, and she scowled outside behind him before closing the door and turning back.

Her office was filled with computer screens, a few running stock numbers and what looked like code. Others were filled with pictures—some he recognized as security clients and others as potential threats. There were always people who wanted them dead, but he both loved and hated that their lives were hanging in the balance. Neutralizing them, the people who intended on bringing harm to their clients or to the family and STEALTH, was one of the best parts of his job.

"Where's your friend?" she asked.

"Huh? Amber?" he asked.

Zoey nodded.

"Oh, I put her up in a cabin. Number eight. Hope that's okay with you."

She nodded. "Yeah, I thought you might." Her voice was unemotional and no matter how long he looked at her, it didn't seem like she was going to give away whether or not she thought his action was a good or bad thing.

"Is that why you called me here?" He ran his hand over his chin, rubbing his stubble. He needed to shave.

It was funny how the mind wandered when it was under a certain level of stress. Though he was sure he wasn't going to get fired—Zoey really did trust and like him—he still didn't like walking into her office without the faintest clue as to why she would call a late meeting.

"What you do with her is on you. That ship—" she waved in the general direction of the police "—has already sailed. We are in on the investigation whether or not we want, now we're just going to have to wait it out. Besides, she seems nice enough. Trustworthy."

A wave of relief washed over him. "Weren't you going to stay out there? Help them out? Or did something happen?"

"Baker made it clear I wasn't to approach the scene, but if it hadn't been for the phone call I received, he could have taken those instructions and stuffed them where the sun doesn't shine."

"I should have told you earlier, but—"

"We've got a problem—besides the remains on the ranch," she said, talking over him.

He nearly bit his tongue. "Where? With whom?" His heart started to thump hard in his chest. *God, I love these moments.*

Zoey pointed toward a computer screen, where there was a mug shot of a man and a bio next to it.

The man had dark brown, midlength hair. Dark eyes. His nose was slightly larger than average. He wasn't smiling in the picture. AJ didn't recognize the man and walked over to the screen, tapping on the bio. The guy was twenty-five, an avid hiker, loved to ski, came from money. His name, Luca Fellini, besides sounding Italian, didn't ring any bells.

"Who is he?" AJ asked.

"Luca Fellini is the son of Frank Fellini."

He shook his head. Nothing.

"Frank is the Italian foreign minister of trade."

"Oh," AJ said. That meant one thing for sure—the guy was going to bring them trouble. Either they were going to fight for him, or against him, but it was going to get dirty.

"An operator working in Rome was sleeping with Luca," Zoey said, giving him an evil smile that spoke of the lengths operatives would go in order to get a job done. "It's amazing what too much wine, a beautiful woman and a little ecstasy can do when you need a man to spill his secrets."

He chuckled, but something about the heady mix made his mind drift to Amber before he pulled himself back to center.

"What did our man Luca say?"

"Do you remember Conflux?"

"Uh, yeah." He laughed.

That was one company he couldn't forget. His brothers Troy and Mike had nearly died working for them a couple of years ago. Conflux was a military engineering company that machined parts for the US government and the different branches of the armed forces. They were worth multimillions and, as such, were an open target for corporate spies. It was one of STEALTH's best clients—there was always guaranteed work.

"And their enemy, Rockwood?"

He nodded. Rockwood had gotten caught sending spies into the belly of the Conflux beast. Their spying had cost them millions, and exposed the fact they were running illicit contracts with foreign nations. They were treasonous bastards.

Bastards who had threatened to take down his family and STEALTH when their team had exposed them, leaving the organization in shreds and in a lot of trouble with the US government.

"What about them?" he growled.

"Since then, we have been running surveillance on the group. We knew these rats would stick their heads back up. It took a while after they took such a big hit, but some of their handiwork is starting to show back up on the dark web."

"And?" The hair rose on the back of his neck.

"Luca, our boy, was talking about his father. The foreign minister. Apparently, he has been buying and selling American military secrets."

"Is the operative running Luca one of ours?" he asked.

"No. She was with the CIA. Unfortunately, she was taken out by Frank when he learned about her relationship with his son."

AJ shuddered. "Those ruthless bastards. I'm sorry to hear about her."

Zoey gave a thin smile. "She didn't go out without a fight. Plus, she is a goddamned hero for her work. She is going to save thousands, if not hundreds of thousands, of servicemen's lives in making the military aware of the data breach. CIA is already looking into it."

He nodded. "So how does this involve us?"

"Luca let it slip that his father was the leader of Rockwood before we took it down. He is trying to resurrect the organization, using it to buy and sell state secrets. According to Luca, his father's number-one mission is to destroy STEALTH. They've put a bounty on our heads."

He would have laughed, but this company had last paid a spy fourteen million dollars to supply them with machining secrets. It made him sick to think about how much they would put out to take down an entire contracting operation like theirs.

"The good news is that they don't know much about STEALTH besides it being a company...except, somehow, they knew the name Spade."

His chest suddenly tightened.

"I need some air," he said as he walked out of Zoey's office. The scent of electronics and dust permeated his senses and clawed at him.

He gulped the night air and looked up at the red lights curling like a whip in the sky.

His family. His entire *family* was in the crosshairs.

They had all been careful in making sure they hadn't left digital trails any more than necessary, but in the social-media age, where facial and voice-recognition software was traded like playing cards on the dark web, they were as good as dead.

That was…*if* they were found.

Kendra had recently been involved in a social-media tit-for-tat deal with a crooked senator and it had blown up, but that was in Missoula. She was now living on the ranch with her fiancé, but according to social media and the web, she was currently residing in New York City.

He did a mental checklist of all the ways their location could be outed as he walked back toward his cabin.

They hadn't been named in any court documents; only false company names had been used. As for anything else…he couldn't think of a way they could be, or had been, exposed.

He was so lost in thought that it wasn't until he was walking in his front door that he even spared a thought for the griz. If it wanted him tonight, it could have had him.

He took off his jacket and threw it over the couch. His beer was sitting on the counter where he had left it. Little beads of condensation were slipping down the brown bottle and the top of the label had started to lift. He was tempted to pick off the paper, like some weird tick, but instead he grabbed the bottle and emptied it with a long drink.

He should have known that between bears, exes and a being so close to a woman he could never have…well, this day was not going to get any better. He just hadn't expected it to fall so dramatically far from grace.

Life had one hell of a way of getting ridiculously complicated in the blink of an eye.

That was all without even taking into consideration their normal everyday running of the teams.

He sighed and pitched the glass bottle into the trash.

Looking in, it had landed next to a cork from a wine bottle. His thoughts moved to Luca and the dead operative.

Too much wine… Zoey's words echoed in his mind.

He didn't even drink wine. Hell, he didn't recall having a bottle in the place. When it came to groceries, he kept the cabin pretty sparse.

Ever so carefully, he reached around behind his back and touched the flesh-warmed grip of his Glock.

He hadn't locked his door when he'd left, but out here there wasn't much of a need. No one got the sneak on this place—at least, no human. There were security systems wired throughout the entire area of the houses, exits and entrances to the ranch.

"Hello?" he called, trying his damnedest not to draw his weapon.

"Yeah…hey, it's just me. I'm out on the back porch."

He recognized Amber's voice and he dropped his hand from his gun. He tried to calm his racing pulse as he slowly walked into his bedroom.

Amber had her arm under her head and a glass of wine in her other hand. She was leaning back in a patio chair, covered with his wool Pendleton blanket, complete with a blue-and-orange geometric pattern. Her blond hair was loose and cascading down and over her shoulders, and ending in curls over the edge of the blanket.

Her nearly *naked* shoulders.

She was so beautiful.

Breathtaking.

Oh, for all that was good in this world. He thanked every single one of his lucky stars as he stared at her and smiled.

He reached up and loosened the top button of his shirt—it seemed to be choking him.

Her skin was so pale, so soft-looking. She was the color of milk and there was a freckle at the top of her left shoulder that begged for his kiss.

"AJ..."

Even the way she spoke his name was creamy and smooth, beckoning for him and the night of fantasies he wanted to fulfill with her.

"Is *this* okay?" She did a tiny motion toward her body with her wineglass. "I know I shouldn't have just borrowed your blanket, but it's cold out here."

He didn't want to point out that she was only wearing a tank top, as her being here was more than okay. It was what he had been thinking about, though not *exactly*, all damn day.

He sat on the chair closest to her, looking at her. "You said you wanted to talk. What's on your mind?"

"You told me if I needed anything, to come talk to you. Did you mean that?" she asked, giving him one of the sexiest looks he had ever seen.

"Absolutely," he said, reaching out and putting his hand gently on the blanket over her knee. "Is everything okay?"

She gave a slight nod. "Yes, I just..." She sighed. "I want you to know that I appreciate you and your team letting me crash here. It's nice." She waved at her surroundings, but her gaze moved to his hand on her.

"You can stay here as long as you need," he said, sending her a gentle smile. Though he was aware that he wasn't offering her a place completely unselfishly, he liked having her here.

"I live alone, sometimes it's pretty quiet. All of the action that happens here, it's a bit refreshing. Though," she said, looking away, "I have to think that a lot of what is happening now with the human remains is directly tied to you and your decision to push everyone back."

"I told you, that was for legal reasons. Nothing more. I thought my asking you here would help prove my intentions were honorable." He frowned. Until he knew for sure the ring on that hand was the one he'd given Tammy... "Don't be offended, but you seem to have a hard time trusting." Not that he could blame her, especially when she had found herself at the literal center of a den of trained killers, but he wasn't about to point that out—this was about her.

"First, I work in a governmental job," she said. "They can be cutthroat."

"Yes, but that's not what I'm sensing here. It's almost as if you were hurt a long time ago."

She stared down at her fingertips as she stretched her hands wide. "My brother died quite a while ago, and it was incredibly hard on my family. In the end, we learned who our real friends were and who the people in our lives were who wanted to tear us down." She paused. "It turns out that there are far more people out there who want to judge you in silence than help."

"I'm so sorry to hear about your brother, Amber." He wasn't sure what else to say, but he loved having her feel safe to open up to him. He liked getting to know more about her and to learn why she worked the way she did.

"It's okay. Like I said, it was a long time ago."

"Time doesn't really matter when it comes to losing the people who you really love. Loss is loss—it changes a person forever."

"Oh, that is one lesson I know all too well." She balled her hands into fists.

There was a glistening in her eyes that made him wonder if she was going to cry. That had been the last thing he'd wanted. "Amber," he said, lifting her chin so he could meet her gaze directly, "I think you are an amazing woman. I know how hard it is to trust, but believe me when I say that I never want to make you hurt." As he took her lips with his, she drew in a breath that was almost like the gasp that came when two bodies melded into one. His body responded, instantly hardened by the gentle touch of her lips against his, mixed with her sexy sound.

Her hand moved up into his hair and she gripped it, just a little roughly, and pulled him harder against her lips. A moan escaped him as she nipped at his bottom lip, gently grazing his skin and beckoning the predator within him to come out and play.

He wanted to kiss her until she couldn't breathe, to reach down and feel the river between her thighs and to taste all that was her. If she let him, he would love to take her to the brink and then some.

"AJ, would you hold me?" she asked, but before the words had even fully left her, he pulled her into his arms.

There was the steady beating of her heart and the warmth of her breath on his skin. It had been so long since he had held a woman like this. A part of him wanted to take this so much further, to let themselves fall into the darkness of the night and let the shadows bring them reprieve from the stark illumination that came with the light of their truths; but ignoring reality didn't keep it from reappearing in the morning.

She leaned back slightly and pressed her lips against his. Their breaths mingled, mixing into a heady storm of want and fear. She broke their kiss, gently pushing him away. "I have to go."

Her words lashed against his soul. "I get it."

He stood up, moving back from her. "I'm sorry for kissing you."

"There are a lot of things you could be sorry for, but kissing me isn't one of them." She smiled up at him as she slipped out of the chair and moved toward the door to leave. "If our situation was different, tonight would be far from over."

Chapter Seven

That was one hell of a night. Amber had not opened herself up to a man like that in a long time, but not an ounce of her regretted her decision. AJ was beyond anything she'd expected. They had definitely taken things to another level. She had wanted to take things further, but was glad that things had ended where they had.

She'd felt silly for asking him to just hold her, but he hadn't hesitated for a moment. He had just pulled her into his arms, and held her tight.

Recalling the sound of his heartbeat made her smile. In theory, it would've been nice to hear it again, but that wasn't what was going to happen. Something like that wouldn't be good for either one of them.

As soon as she got the bear, she was done here. He knew that just as well as she did.

Yeah, they could call each other and text

and do all the cutesy things that people in relationships did, but they were both so busy it
would never work.

He had been gone for nearly an hour last
night. Though she had seen him go into the
ranch house, she didn't know what had been
going on; for all she knew, he'd been ordering
hits on people. She laughed at the thought as
she laced up her boots.

The deputy had told her what they did for a
living and he had vaguely explained it as well,
but last night AJ definitely didn't seem like the
kind of guy who was an assassin. Not hardly.
He was sweet and giving. If asked, she'd hon-
estly have to say that he was one of the best
kissers she had experienced. She could only
imagine how good he would be when they actually had sex. Maybe that was reason enough
not to go there. If they did, she wasn't sure that
she could leave it at a one-night stand.

After getting ready for the day in her cabin
and making herself a steaming cup of coffee,
she went outside and got into her truck. AJ's
lights were still off and it didn't look like he
was up yet, surprisingly.

He didn't seem like the type who would
sleep in, but he had put in some time on her.

She smiled wildly at the thought.

Yes, keeping this to a one-time thing was already going to be a challenge.

Hopefully the bear trap was sprung and she could spend the rest of the day figuring out the logistics in getting the biologists and her team out here to help her relocate the animal.

Thinking about that... She needed to do a little digging. Part of her was tempted to sit out in her rig and work. If she waited, she might get to see AJ when he came out to go to work, but then again, she didn't want to risk falling back into his arms. She had already self-rescued from those arms once. If she fell back in, work wouldn't be getting done—at least not the kind that got her paid.

As it was, his lights weren't even on. She had a few minutes to get some work done before hitting the road.

She popped open her laptop and signed in to work. If she had to guess, there would be phone calls all day.

At least hunting season was over—that would limit the number of random calls that would come in from people wanting to report trespassing and the like. However, there were a few poaching calls that her deputies would need to continue digging into in order to solve and prosecute.

She pulled up her email. There were forty sitting in there from yesterday and twenty-three from just today. She had been thinking she would beat everyone to their proverbial desks this morning. Nothing appeared as if it needed her immediate attention, so she turned her focus to what she was looking for—collared grizzly-bear locations.

The locations were exact, but sometimes the data was slow to upload, with approximately a three-day lag. Sometimes, if a bear was in certain areas, the data signal wouldn't even be attainable, but hopefully she could get a general idea.

Last year, they'd had a bear, Lingenpolter, that had been caught in a culvert trap—like the one they had set last night—and had been relocated more than two hundred miles to the north, near Glacier Park. In less than two months, the bear traveled more than five hundred miles in a zigzag pattern and had last pinged farther south than where they had originally caught him. It was incredible just how far and wide a male could travel.

If the bear on the ranch was a male, it very well may have been traveling through when it found food and holed up. If it was female, or a sow with cubs—which there hadn't been any evidence of—it would be another story entirely. She could very well den up near the ranch and move in to the territory. Meaning, the Spades and the Martins would be dealing with her for years to come.

Amber pulled up the latest report of GPS readouts of collared bears. The information was from last week, and if she added three days to that... She pulled together a general geofence for the area.

There were four known possibilities—three females and a male.

Those were just the ones that had been caught and collared. If the reported sightings were to be believed, more than a dozen grizzly bears could have been the one that was visiting the ranch.

Based on the probabilities, she had to assume it was a female.

She clicked on bear number 832. It was, approximately, a twenty-nine-year-old sow griz who had originally been captured and tagged in a drainage twenty miles to the east. The girl had been chomping on a farmer's chickens, then hit the garbage inside a neighbor's garage, which led to her capture and tagging. They had moved her north, but like Lingenpolter, she had eventually picked her way back to the general area. Her epic adventure wasn't as much of a zigzag as the boar's, but she had steadily come back to what she no doubt thought of as home.

Amber couldn't blame the bear, but if that was the one that they were dealing with—one that had been somewhat habituated to people and the food sources they provided and was now back looking for more—it could prove fatal for the sow. They had to have a somewhat rigid policy; a habituated bear was a dangerous one.

If this was the bear seen out here, it was very likely that the woman whose hand they'd found had fallen victim to a bad bear.

Amber was torn. She wanted to hope that the bear hadn't killed the woman, but had only scavenged, given the alternative—both for the woman and the bear.

There was already enough of a target on grizzly bears; much of the public wanted to pull them off the endangered-species list and start to allow for an active hunting season on the predators. A woman being killed would definitely draw more strength to the case.

From a conservation perspective, predators needed to be controlled or it would lead to massive swings in predators and prey. She'd rather it be steady instead of bears overloading the balance and turning to unhealthy practices that left her holding the scale.

There was a knock on the driver-side door of her truck and she jerked back from her computer. AJ was standing outside her window, holding two cups of coffee from Starbucks.

"Oh, hey," she said, rolling down her window. She was both excited and embarrassed at seeing him.

AJ smiled at her. He was nearly irresistible when he gave her that look. "Sorry to surprise you—that wasn't my intention." He handed her the venti cup. "It's just a regular latte with sweetener, I didn't know what you liked."

"That was really thoughtful of you." She took the coffee and pulled the stopper from the cup, then took a long sip. The coffee wasn't very hot. "Is there even a Starbucks around here?"

He shrugged. "Not really, but there are a few in the city. I ran in there about an hour ago. After you left I couldn't really sleep…" There was a tug of sadness in his voice.

Or maybe she was just hearing things. If he was upset with her, he wouldn't have been bringing her coffee—a coffee that had taken almost an hour to get. He really was a good man.

Before she could allow herself to think about the likeable parts of him, she needed to focus. Here came the awkwardness.

She sighed. "About last night—"

He shook his head and from the pinched look on his face, he wanted her to stop.

Good. We have an understanding.

She smiled with relief and she could feel her body relax.

"You going up to check the trap? If you are, I'll come along and show you around the ranch a little. Maybe we can track the bear a bit more and see where it's been going."

He stood quietly by her window for a moment, sipping on his coffee. She squirmed slightly, but really...what did it hurt if he was by her side today? If they were in the truck, working, there wouldn't really be much time for any type of shenanigans to happen.

Besides, they had an unspoken *understanding*.

"I'd be happy to have you along." She did enjoy his company.

He gave her a quick nod and made his way around to the passenger seat. "I talked to Zoey this morning. There's a sheriff's deputy keeping an eye on the scene. They tried to stay out of the way of your trap, and inside their car all night. I expect that the full investigation team will probably be here in the next couple of hours to go over the entire area."

"Yeah, I don't expect that anybody wanted to rush around in the woods last night with just a skeleton crew when there's a grizzly around. I certainly didn't advise it."

"Is there a chance we can put more traps out?" he asked.

"We have one more trap that's available, but it's in Kalispell. If we don't get a hit on this trap, we can start thinking about it." She paused. "It's my hope, though, that this bear just moved on and isn't a continuing problem."

He grimaced slightly, like he didn't totally agree with her, but instead of thinking too much about his reaction, she turned back to the road.

"Baker and his team canvased a small area and collected the hand last night. They didn't find any other remains. They dropped the hand off at the medical examiner's office already. According to Zoey, they were going to pull some fingerprints." The pinched expression on his face seemed to intensify as he spoke.

"That's good. At least we can get an ID on the remains. I always like bringing closure to families. Even if they learn their loved ones are dead, it is better than living with the agony of not knowing what has happened to someone you care about." Her thoughts moved to her brother.

He cocked his head, studying her. "You say that like you've been through something like that."

It hadn't been her intention to open up this can of worms with him, or with anyone. "What happened in the past doesn't matter. There is only moving forward."

"Mmm-hmm," he said, not sounding satisfied in her dismissal of the subject. "Do you like being a game warden?"

She was grateful he was changing the subject as she slowly made her way toward the trap. "It can be rewarding, but challenging," she said, smiling.

"I bet it's a really fun job."

"It certainly can be. Some people think we are more like law enforcement than anything, but I like to look at our profession like we are conservators of the natural resources. We protect Montana for generations to come."

He nodded, but she could tell from the way he was staring in the direction of the location of the remains that his mind was somewhere else. Of course, he would've been more concerned with the comings and goings of the ranch instead of their little interlude. No wonder he hadn't wanted to talk about it this morning. She was as much relieved as she was slightly hurt.

She shouldn't have been hurt, though, since this was exactly what she wanted. Ambivalence.

"You have any idea when the crime lab will be done with their tests?" she asked. AJ didn't look away from the window and merely shrugged.

She had a sense he'd been hiding something since yesterday, but she wasn't sure it was appropriate to ask or not. She didn't want him to be offended, but her curiosity was getting the better of her. "Is there any way you would know who the hand belonged to?" AJ tensed. She could tell he was making an effort to not look at her.

"Odd, Detective Baker asked me the same question last night." He paused, looking away from her. "Just know everything that has been happening in the last twenty-four hours is way outside my comfort zone."

Everything?

If he thought the kiss, being held by him, was inside of her comfort zone, well, he had another think coming.

On the other hand, maybe he was just focused on work and not on their growing feelings toward one another. Or maybe he meant exactly what he'd said, but in a *good* way— like he wasn't the kind of guy who expected or had experienced brief interludes.

Was it his way of saying that he wanted more?

No. She took a breath and tried to pull herself back to the moment. *I'm overthinking this. It's just this, riding in a truck, nothing more.*

As they made it to the trap, she stopped the truck and put it in Park. From where they sat, she could see that the gate was still open and it hadn't been tripped. No bear.

Farther down the road was a cruiser. In the front was a deputy, his head tilted back in sleep. She chuckled at the sight, but she didn't begrudge the guy. She'd never taken a nap out in the woods when she had been on duty, but it would have been easy when a person was on their own in the peaceful timber.

Unfortunately, if this guy was caught sleeping on duty, it could very well spell the end of his career—the politics in law enforcement and in being a game warden could be brutal and unforgiving. "Should we wake him up?" she asked, sending AJ a malicious grin.

"It would be the thoughtful thing," he said with a chuckle. "If I caught one of my team members doing this, they would be in deep."

With her lights off, she drove up to the cruiser and let her truck roll into the front bumper of the guy's car. The deputy woke with a start, grabbing the wheel like he thought he had fallen asleep while driving. He stared out at them for a long second before seemingly coming to his senses and realizing what he had just been caught doing and by whom. A guilty smile erupted over his features.

She laughed as she backed up her pickup and then stopped by the guy and rolled down her window. "Hey," she said, a smile on her lips.

"Morning," the deputy said, looking from her to AJ like he was hoping against hope that neither of them was from his department. "You caught me studying there."

"Yeah, we noticed." She chuckled. "How long have you been sitting out here?"

The guy looked down at his watch. "They had me roll out here about six hours ago. It was overtime for me, so… You know how it goes."

The guy was definitely embarrassed. In an attempt to mollify his embarrassment and guilt, and any underlying concern for his job and reputation, she had to throw him a bone. "Definitely. As for studying, we didn't see anything." She winked.

AJ tipped his fingers in the man's direction, reiterating her statement.

The guy perked up. "Sounds like this is a really interesting case. Baker told me a bit about it. You guys helping with the search today?"

That hadn't exactly been her plan.

"I'm not sure if we are. We have a bear to locate," AJ said, but he rubbed awkwardly at the back of his neck. "You know what area they covered last night?"

He had said he'd talked this through with

Zoey this morning, so she was surprised he was asking the deputy questions. Yet, maybe he was verifying the information or hoping for more.

"They just worked the direct area last night. Inside the tape there," the deputy said, pointing at the yellow tape that was tied up in a makeshift square around the area where they had located the hand. "Any sign of your griz?"

She shook her head. She wasn't exactly sure what AJ had up his sleeve, but she had a feeling part of him was struggling with what had happened last night…just like she was. She quelled the urge to be annoyed as she tried to be vague and relaxed.

AJ seemed to have noticed the shift in her demeanor and he reached over and gently touched the tips of his fingers to her leg, silently reassuring her without drawing attention from the deputy. "I'm thinking we are going to go up the hill a ways, see if we can find any more signs. Let us know when the incident commander or detective arrives and maybe we can link up."

The deputy gave them a stiff nod. "Will do, and let me know if you find anything. I'll be here until they arrive."

They pulled away from the deputy and she made sure to close her window before speaking. Opening her mouth, she tried to think of the exact right words to navigate this, but none came. She wanted to reprimand him for including her in his offer, but she wasn't actually upset and it would only push him away. Though, that would be better in some ways. It would make her internal struggle that much easier to ignore.

Chapter Eight

Amber was trying to be cool as she kept driving along the bumpy road, but every thought she had was about AJ kissing her. If she was this caught up with merely a kiss, maybe it was good she'd left before they could have taken things any further.

"I pulled some information about the bears that are known to be traveling in the area," she said, finally deciding to avoid anything but their immediate needs. "I'm thinking if we can find the place where it came through your fence line, we might be able to get a hair sample and run the DNA. If it is one of the bears on file, we can at least get a better idea of what we are dealing with—if this bear is going to be more of a problem or not."

AJ nodded. "We have sensors on our fences. I can have Zoey send me a GPS pin of any recent activity." He pulled out his phone and sent a quick text.

She was used to tech, but this was extra cool; though, it reminded her of just how out of her element she really was with this family and this man.

He pointed ahead. "Up here, the road is going to split and then there will be a cattle guard and gate." He clicked away on his phone, looking over a map.

"How many acres do you guys have here?"

He shrugged. "Thousands. I don't know exactly. Zoey doesn't really talk about it a whole lot. It seems huge, though." He pointed at the mountain to their left. "This all abuts public land, though, so it makes it feel infinitely bigger." He turned to her, looking up from his phone for a second. "And, hey, I'm glad you agreed to let me come along today."

She shook her head and waved him off as if the thought hadn't already crossed her mind. "It's no big deal. The nice part about my job is that I have a lot of flexibility as long as I keep my superiors happy. Besides, we need to make sure you and your teams are safe. I have to admit—" she smiled "—it is intriguing to be working with a death investigation. Normally, I just report the bodies and go. It's interesting to get to be involved in the whole process." She hadn't known that was exactly how she felt until the words rolled out of her, and in them she found her truth.

He nodded and turned back to his phone. "I'm glad to hear that you aren't just out here for me."

There went any good feelings that she was starting to have about working with him. *Poof. Gone.*

With it went some of the awkwardness she was feeling with him. *Good. Work, it was.*

"You have a job, same as I do. We are both just trying to do the best for our employers and the communities that rely on us." She pulled to a stop at the gate. There was a lock with a number code.

His face fell slightly, but he turned away from her as he got out of the truck and unlocked the gate. The cattle guard rattled as she drove over it and waited for him to close the gate and lock it behind them.

"The pin Zoey sent me, the one she thinks might be where the bear has been moving through, is just another mile or so up the road." He seemed to have let their earlier point go and she was all too happy about it.

There was silence between them until he motioned for her to pull over. "The fence is this way," he said, motioning toward the west.

The snow was thick and heavy, the kind

that fell on warmer days, and it crunched and squeaked under her feet as they started to descend into the timber.

Her mind wandered to the Inuit. They had more than fifty words for snow. No doubt, there would be one for this kind, one that would stick around and get covered with the light, powdery snow of brutal winter days, all while acting like a blanket for the world beneath. Protector and base...permanently impermanent. She didn't know all the words, but the term *matsaaruti* came to mind. It was the type of snow that would freeze to their sled runners when they were mushing.

She kicked at the snow, harder than she'd intended, and it flew up, with a few of the pieces smacking AJ in the back.

He turned and stared at her. "What was that?" he asked, giving her a playful look.

"I... I didn't mean..." Instead of continuing and admitting she hadn't meant to hit him, she reached down and made a snowball. She pitched it at him, hitting him in the middle of the chest.

"What the...?" he said with a laugh. He grabbed some snow and chucked it in her direction. It stuck to her coat.

She laughed as she walked up beside him, brushing the remnants of snow from her jacket before reaching over and brushing the wet bits of snow from his back. The muscles on his back were hard and tense as she touched them and she quickly dropped her hand.

As they started to walk again, with her by his side, she was struck by how badly she wanted him to reach over and hold her hand.

They walked for ten minutes or so. There were little birds that looked like shrikes flitting from tree to tree, and as the sun worked its way up in the sky, there was the occasional creak of a branch and a thump of snow as it slipped from its hold and hit the ground.

Every day in the woods was a damn good day. She didn't get to spend nearly the amount of time hiking as she would have liked.

In the distance, she spotted a barbed-wire fence. The fence posts were still the tawny color of freshly treated wood.

"Zoey said an animal triggered the system in this stretch. Could be fifty feet or so from this point—it's not super exact." He motioned toward the fence.

She nodded, not wanting to tell him that this was far more exact than anything she had done to this effect in the past. Usually, if she was trying to collect hair samples, she would end up walking for miles trying to find the place where the animal may or may not have come through a fence. More often than not, she came up empty-handed. It turned out having him come along was a good thing.

"I bet you work poaching cases a lot," he began as they walked up the fence line, looking for a place that would be bent or pushed down by a bear moving over the wire.

She wasn't sure why he brought it up or what made him think about it, but she nodded. "Yep, right now we have a case where we think a guy killed ten deer and three elk. Left the animals, took the antlers."

"Oh, that kind of thing pisses me off. People do know they can just *buy* antlers, right?"

"No kidding, but to some of these people it's not really about the acquisition of a food source or even really about the antlers, instead it is an act of rebellion. It is a way for them to act out against the government. You know, 'no one controls them' kind of mentality."

"I can only imagine," he said with an annoyed grumble. "How do you even catch them?"

"Nowadays, it's a lot easier than in the past. Just a couple years ago, though, someone shot a bear and took its paws and gallbladder before leaving the rest. Fortunately for us, where they had stepped out of their truck and shot, they had dropped an ATM receipt. Made it pretty easy to track them down." She smiled victoriously.

"Damn." He chuckled. "That's almost as good as them literally leaving you a business card."

"Actually, it made freezing their assets that much easier." She smiled. "Turned out they had been dealing in exotic animals and parts on the black market. That one felt damned good to take down."

"That is awesome. I know the feeling you are talking about, when you get to do the right things for the right reasons and end up making a difference. Feels *damned* good." He stopped walking, but she moved ahead.

She looked down the fence line. A couple of posts from where she was, she caught sight of a bent top wire. Stuffed into several barbs were what looked like tufts of brown fur. She rushed up to the spot. Sure enough, it was hair. Better, it was the coarse, kinky hair of a bear, not the more straight, hollow kind of the herbivores in the area.

They had just struck gold.

"AJ, look!" she called back to him excitedly.

Instead of hurrying to her side as she expected, he was staring down at his phone.

"AJ?" she asked, worried. "Is everything okay?"

He didn't look up; instead, it was like he hadn't even heard her speaking.

"AJ?" she called, this time a little bit louder.

Finally, he glanced up, his face hard and his eyes a bit unfocused, his mind elsewhere. "Huh? Yeah?"

"Is everything okay?" she asked again.

Her question seemed to pull him back to the moment. "Yeah," he said, slightly shaking his head. "I'm fine. It's all good. What did you find?"

She pointed at the top wire. "We found it. We found hair. We are hopefully going to get answers."

He huffed, saying something just under his breath. She wasn't entirely sure, but she could have sworn he'd said, "At least one of us will."

Chapter Nine

AJ wasn't exactly thrilled as they made their way back to the ranch house. He had really been hoping that they wouldn't find anything up there on the hill. If anything, he had been counting on them being out there in the woods all day, searching for something that they would never find but would keep them away from people and the intrigue that was swirling around the place.

The thought of being around a death investigation that was likely tied to Tammy threatened to break his heart. If they learned it was her, he wasn't sure that he could keep his composure. Besides, he had Rockwood's threat looming heavily over their heads and both that and the field trip gave him something else to concentrate on besides that ache in his chest.

Now, thanks to the text from Baker, he was even more leery to head back. According to the detective, he was hoping to meet with AJ this afternoon. Apparently, though he was taking the lead on the case, he wasn't on the ranch but was having his team run the search patterns instead. Which meant one of two things—either he had gotten a positive ID on the victim, and had tracked the ring and was now looking to question him about his role in it being found on the ranch, or the detective just didn't want to have a part in the actual digging through snow and ice in hopes of finding more remains. AJ hoped for the latter.

"Where do we need to run the hair?" he asked, turning to Amber.

She took off her hat and threw it on the dashboard. She let out her ponytail, her hair falling over her shoulders…reminding him all too much of kissing her last night, holding her.

His body jerked to life, but he tried to control the response. He had done very well in pretending like nothing had gone on last night.

It was fine. He didn't want a real relationship. She was a good woman and she made him laugh, but that wasn't going to be enough. Just like Tammy, Amber would want compromises from him and his life that he couldn't make—not as team leader and not as the man he was. He was all in on this life. A heart couldn't have love for a woman and the kind of work he did.

His thoughts moved to his siblings and the Martins. They had found love and relationships, proving him a bit wrong, but they weren't working in the same role that he found himself in. Sure, Zoey was married, but the work had to be taxing on both her husband and her kiddo.

If he went back to working directly in the field and had to take on a more active trigger-pulling role instead of just overseeing the operation, he didn't want to have a woman or family back at home to worry about him. It wasn't fair.

He had been the man coming to the door to tell a wife her husband had died far too many times and he never wanted anyone else to have to bear that duty for him.

Yes, arm's length or farther was even better.

"The lab for the hair is in Missoula, at the university." She smiled over at him, and it made his heart both shift and ache in his chest. "It shouldn't take too long for me to get the answer."

He nodded. "Then what?"

"Based on the bear, we go from there. If it's not a problem bear, we will continue to try and trap. I'm thinking about moving the trap closer to where we found the hair, but just because we found hair there doesn't mean it will move through that exact area again."

"What if it is a trouble bear?"

She pinched her lips. "Then we may have to make a harder choice than just trapping and relocating. We may need to take down the bear and do a necropsy to find if it was ingesting the person whose hand we found."

"It's a woman, by the way." He tapped on his phone.

"Was that the text you got up there? Confirmation of some kind? I didn't want to ask, but you seemed really bothered."

"Baker wants a meeting later," he said with a grumble. "I can only imagine what he wants to chat about."

She gave him a side-eye. "He just wants to talk to you, or with your whole crew?"

From the sounds of things, she had the same gut reaction to a detective asking for a meeting as he did. That didn't bode well.

"Just me."

She gave him a long look, reading him, and he hated every second of it. "Is there something you should tell me, AJ? Something I don't know?"

He wanted to tell her about the ring, about Tammy, about everything, but in doing so... after last night. *Gah.*

AJ ran his hands over his face—he didn't know where to start. "This is turning into more than I ever expected or bargained for. Thank goodness Baker is a friend."

"What does that mean?" She slowed down the truck, but she pulled past the ranch house and headed toward Missoula.

This was going to be a long drive to the city.

"It's a long story." He gave a long exhale. "I was engaged before. A couple years or so ago."

Amber shifted in her seat and he noticed her gripping the steering wheel incrementally tighter. "Oh?"

She didn't lead him. He appreciated she wasn't pushing him to tell her more than he was ready to in this moment, but at the same time, he wished she would give him a clue as to how much she wanted to know.

"Yes, I was engaged to a woman from New Jersey. She was a total city girl."

Amber started to laugh. "You?" She looked down at his boots and Wranglers. "Did she have a thing for cowboys or something? How did you get hooked up with her?"

"First, we haven't always lived on this ranch. My family's company was bought out by STEALTH, and we moved here to be a part of their group. We haven't really been here that long."

"Now, that—you not being here long—I did know. Where are you originally from?"

He answered with a tired smile. "Contracting kids are a bit like military kids—home is where your family is, it's not a place."

"That's not a bad way to live," she said, but there wasn't conviction in her voice.

"Yes, I loved it. I lived in Belgium and Africa, just about the A to Z of countries. I don't even think I could name them all." He stopped from going too deeply into his history. That would lead to thinking about the shadows in his mind where all the dark thoughts and deeds lingered like ghosts. "I met her when I was twenty-five and we dated long-distance for a while. Then she hinted it was time."

"Time for what?"

"You know. Get married or break up." He shrugged.

"You do know that an ultimatum never leads to anything good, especially if we are talking about marriage."

"Ha," he said, "don't I know that."

"But you still asked her to marry you?"

He ran his hand over his face again. "There were a lot of things changing in my life at that point. Company's future was up in the air and everyone's jobs depended on me. Getting engaged was the easiest choice. Though, I didn't really ask her."

"You *didn't ask her*?" She furrowed her brow. "How does one get engaged without someone asking them the question?"

He let out a gut-deep laugh. "We were walking through a little town with a jeweler and she walked in. I followed her. We ended up designing a ring for her. A few months later, she picked it up from the place and she just never took it off of her ring finger."

"Did you guys talk about being engaged?" Amber asked, as they rolled down the highway toward the city.

"She did. I guess I didn't say anything. So pretty soon it was just a thing. We started planning the wedding and the honeymoon. Unfortunately, my schedule never really allowed for time off. Not then. She didn't like it. She didn't support who I was or what I wanted." He ran his hand over his throat as if just the mere thought of those days threatened to suffocate him.

Amber sighed.

He paused. "Sorry. I didn't mean to talk about her like that." They'd been so young, and neither of them could be blamed for knowing what they wanted...or didn't want. "Clearly, though, it didn't work out between us. It wasn't a pretty breakup. Then I moved to Montana. She tried to talk to me a few times after we broke things off, but no. Just *no*."

Amber glanced at him after a moment. "Have you talked to her lately?"

He tried to think of the last time he had actually responded to one of her calls or texts. "She texted me a few months ago, but I didn't respond. I know she tried to contact Kendra, but my sister would have none of it. I think there were four-letter words exchanged."

He was glad to see a flicker of satisfaction flash over Amber's face. "Did your family not really like her?"

"Meh," he said with a shrug. "They were fine with it—they didn't really want me to get married to her. Yet, they are my family so they went along with the idea. They always support my decisions when it comes to my personal life, but that doesn't mean that they go along with my plans warmly."

"I can see that being a problem with them," she said, tapping her fingers on the wheel. "The united front, like what they presented the detective and I with, can be a bit intimidating."

"Oh." He chuckled. "That wasn't anything. We can be far more unapproachable when we need to be."

She smiled at that admission, but there seemed

to be a look of disapproval there, too. "Tammy didn't fit," he continued. "She said she understood what we did, accepted it, but when the rubber hit the road and she was asked to accommodate, it didn't work. That sealed the deal when it came to my family disliking her."

"I definitely understand what having an unconventional job can do to a person's personal life…or, in my case, lack thereof. Long-term relationships are too much work, so sometimes it's easier to ward off *all* relationships."

He wanted to reach over, take her hand and tell her that what he really wanted was a woman just like her—independent, strong, smart, beautiful, soft and a touch brutal when life required it.

Admitting all of that to her would only make it harder when it came to the kiss he was trying to forget. It had been nice, but that was where things needed to stop. To ask for anything more from her or from their situation was only opening the door to pain and not possibilities. He'd learned to be skeptical of love, all thanks to Tammy.

"Right now, I don't know about having a woman in my life." He wasn't sure if he should rip off the Band-Aid or gently tug at the edges when it came to the topic of their situation. "I guess I'm a little gun-shy about jumping into anything. You can see how well it worked for me last time." He laughed nervously.

She sighed and nodded. "I have had some of the same issues in relationships. Not imposed engagements, but significant others that wanted more than I could give. Being in the jobs we are in, I think it's impossible to find someone who *gets it*. I'm going to be gone sometimes. Especially during the hunting season, and I can't say that I've had a relationship that has stood that test. A man wants a woman who can be there in the night—every night."

"Exactly."

"I can't even imagine what it would be like with both people having jobs like ours," she said, looking over at him. "We probably wouldn't even end up seeing each other in the day, let alone the nights."

How did that adage go…? Death by a thousand paper cuts. Yeah, that may have been preferable right now. He shouldn't have been feeling or thinking about any of these things when all they needed to do was find a bear, and then she would move on to the next call… and disappear from his life.

Thankfully, before they could go any deeper

into their nonplausible relationship, they pulled up to the Skaggs Building at the university.

"Do you want to run the hair samples in with me? It may take a few minutes. I'm going to try and see if they can push things through a little quicker than normal, given the circumstances."

AJ's phone pinged in his hand. "Nah, it's okay. You go do your thing. I'll wait out here for you and answer some emails." He lifted his phone for her to see, just as the phone's screen lit up with another message. "It's definitely going to be a workday."

"I get it," she said. "I'll leave the keys in, so you start the truck and keep warm if you like. I'll be as quick as I can, but give me fifteen or so."

He nodded. "Take your time."

She grabbed her hat and put it on, then grabbed her bag and got out. She gave him a little wave as she turned and started to walk toward the large brown building at the edge of the parking lot.

He couldn't help but watch her army green pants stretch over her ass as she walked away. It was hardly the first time he had stared at her ass today, but it was magnetic. She was so sexy. His mouth watered as his thoughts slipped back to last night and how her body had felt in his arms. Hell, she had even tasted perfect.

There was the vibration of his phone, pulling him back just as she stepped behind a line of cars and out of view.

He should have gone with her, but he really did have a list of things to handle this morning. None more pressing than hoping that Baker didn't have anything on him, at least not yet.

Clicking on the screen, he opened up his messenger. Kendra had started texting an hour ago. As their attorney, she needed the truth, and he had made sure to tell her about his seeing the ring and assuming it was Tammy's. She hadn't given away a single spark of emotion at the news. He appreciated that about her—she was all business when she needed to be, and he could trust her to keep things at a professional level. As for everyone else knowing his secret…he had to keep it close to the vest. Even Kendra agreed.

He clicked on her picture. It was a long text, but she reiterated that he wasn't to answer any condemning questions without her present. He knew the game, but it was nice to have a sister who always had his back, legally.

He was going to return her text, but before he had the chance, his phone rang. "Hello?"

"You won't believe it." Kendra sounded breathless, like she had been running.

"What? What's going on?"

"I did a little digging. Tammy had been staying in Missoula. She had a hotel room at the Red Lion."

"Oh…" His stomach dropped, landing somewhere near his boots on the dirty floor mat of the pickup. Tammy had been in Missoula. That meant…the hand could have very well been hers. Kendra, no doubt, knew that just as well as he did. He hated being so unsure of everything, but prepared for the worst-case scenario. For once it would be nice to have some clearly defined answers.

"Are you around this morning?"

"At the ranch? No. I'm in the city with Amber."

"I'm not saying you should meddle in a police investigation, but ideally I would love a peek at the footage from the hotel."

"I don't think it's a great idea if I go anywhere near Tammy's last known location."

"I'm aware," Kendra said, sounding slightly annoyed, "but it would be damned nice to know if she is still standing or not. I don't want you to walk into your meeting with Baker tonight without us knowing exactly what he is going to bring to the table…at least as far as findings."

"You know what I say about going into anything blind," he said, his voice low.

Kendra huffed. "Unless we find out what Tammy had going on…yeah, we are both going to be as good as dead."

Chapter Ten

Amber gave the tech at the lab one last wave before making her way back to her truck, where AJ was waiting—hopefully, that was. Though he had opened up to her about his ex—whom she still wasn't sure why he had brought up—she couldn't help feeling like their growing closer wasn't the best idea. To reveal everything about herself would only draw focus on how different they really were. He was a worldly man with the power to effect wars around the globe while she spent most of her days traveling around the state helping animals.

When he figured out how far apart they were, he would pull away and she would be left in the tailings of his affection. As such, she couldn't open up anymore.

Acknowledging the rationality of her thoughts, she couldn't help the grin that erupted over her features when she spotted AJ talking on his phone, waiting for her.

He had finally opened up to her about his life, and, of course, it was just when they had gotten to the university. How did that kind of thing always seem to happen? Did men just wait for the most inopportune moment to speak their minds, or did it just seem like it was too late, because there was never enough time to ask all the questions that were swirling through her mind? It had to be the latter.

In this case, though, she wasn't sure what she should or shouldn't ask. AJ was a man with secrets, some of which she wasn't sure she wanted to know.

He looked up and their eyes connected. Dipping his head in acknowledgment, he sent her an exhausted smile. Hopefully the tired look in his eyes wasn't there because of her. He had said it was a workday. She knew all too well what that could entail in her world; she couldn't even begin to imagine what all that would mean for a man whose profession and employees spanned the globe.

She slowed down, politely waiting for him to end his phone call before making her way to the truck.

There was a strain in his face, but his eyes widened as he watched her get in. Regardless of what she was feeling and they were saying— or not saying—he liked her. She could sense it in the way he looked at her and the way his body moved toward her when she settled into her seat. There was definitely a pull of some kind between them.

In fact, that was exactly how it had felt when he had been kissing her. She could definitely go for feeling his tongue on hers again.

She clenched her thighs together, tight, as she tried to make the blood rush back up to her brain because clearly, she wasn't thinking with the right part of her body. Work first.

"How'd it go in there?" AJ asked, motioning toward the Skaggs Building.

"It was fine. They said they could get us the test results pretty quick. Less than seventy-two hours."

He nodded like he was thoroughly impressed. "I had no idea they could move it through that fast."

"The tech said their lab could do it in seventy-two. It just depends on what all they have in the system."

"That is pretty amazing." He scratched at his freshly shaven chin for a moment, like he was thinking. "Do you need to take any other calls today?"

She shook her head. "Nope. I need to put up some signs and work through some cases and get statements, but there is nothing that is pressing."

"Could you drop me back at the ranch? I don't expect you to put up with me all day." His words were clearly meant to show that he was being thoughtful, but there was an air to them that made her question if he was just trying to get rid of her. Which was ridiculous, since he'd offered to shadow her today. Had she said something? Or maybe not enough when he'd spoken about his ex…

She kept her tone neutral in an attempt not to sound hurt as she said, "Yeah, I can run you back."

He didn't respond as she started the truck. He was still looking at his phone, like he had been earlier.

"Everything okay?" she asked.

He sighed, glancing up at her. "Not really… I'm stuck. I don't know what to do here."

His admission caught her off guard. The man, the team leader and boss, was letting her in to a moment when *he* didn't know what to do. She was flattered but she tried to play it cool. "What's going on?"

He scrunched his eyes shut and reached up and scratched under the brim of his white cowboy hat. "So, I just got a call."

"Oh?" She sat back in her seat, watching for

cars behind them, but not going anywhere for a minute. "What's up?"

"It was Kendra. You know Tammy? My ex?"

"Kendra is the attorney, right?"

"Yeah."

"Why would she call you about your ex?" And then it hit her. Tammy hadn't just randomly come up in their conversation. Suddenly, the ring on the hand they'd found flashed into her mind. It wasn't that he was trying to deepen their relationship, he was telling her secrets... Secrets that his family was involved in and helping to conceal. "AJ, whose hand was that on the ranch?"

His face turned white. "To be honest, I don't know." There was a long, drawn-out silence. She didn't dare speak. "It is a woman's hand. Like I said."

"But?" She tried not to spit out the word, but there was no stopping.

"The ring on that hand... I've tried to tell myself it wasn't Tammy's, but... That ring... It's probably her engagement ring."

Chapter Eleven

Just like that. His secret was out and now Amber would be out, too. It was too bad. They'd only just met, and yet something about her had calmed him. Both last night and again today, despite his world feeling like it was starting to fall around him, her presence had been a comfort.

They were silent for the next fifteen minutes as she sat in the truck next to him, unmoving except for the occasional slow blinking of her eyes and her steady breathing.

This was purgatory.

Finally, she turned to him, their gazes meeting. "I think it's best if I take you back to your ranch."

His stomach, somewhere already on the truck's mat, sank even lower. "I'm sorry, Amber." There was a quake in his voice. "I should have told you right away, but I was hoping that ring wasn't the same one. I still am."

"You knew the moment you saw it. You

chose to keep the secret from me." She was deadly calm as she spoke, and it was more terrifying than if she had been screaming. When he didn't respond, she continued in that tone. "Everything you have done since you met me has been calculated, and—"

"Whoa. No. That's absolutely not true. I just…"

"It's okay. You don't owe me anything. You don't owe me an explanation now, either. You did what you did, and I can guess why. I don't need tired excuses or justifications." She made her way out onto the road.

"Amber… Please, don't," he begged. "I'm so sorry."

She lifted her hand, beckoning him to stop.

There was no doubt in his mind that if he didn't take this chance, riding with her back to the ranch, that he wouldn't get another to make up for what he had done. She was right, though. He had made the choice to keep her in the dark.

"I know you say you understand why I did what I did, but just know… I didn't want it to be her hand out there." He sucked in a long breath before continuing. "And I promise, on my mother's grave, that I didn't have anything to do with it being on our property. I'm still hoping it's not her hand. Yet, the fact that Detective Baker wants to talk to me... I'm thinking that it's probably her...that they've got a positive ID. It's eating me up."

Amber cringed at his words. "You swear... You absolutely *promise* that you didn't have a thing to do with hurting her?"

He nodded and put his hand over his heart in sincerity. "Amber, I promise."

Her shoulders relaxed and she slowed the truck down. "When was the last time you talked to her, really?"

He shrugged. "Like I told you before, months ago. She had texted and called, but I didn't respond."

"But she has your phone number?"

"She does. Tammy and I ended on a crappy note, but that doesn't mean I hated her or that I wished anything but the best for her."

Amber pursed her lips. If anything, she seemed torn. That, he could understand. He reached over and put out his hand, palm up, offering himself to her. "Amber, I wasn't using you. I wasn't keeping you in the dark on purpose. I just... I was *stupid*."

She hesitated for a moment, but then reached over and took his hand. "Please, promise me one thing..." she said, begging him with a look. "No more secrets."

He tensed. "Amber, my world is all secrets,

but I will promise that I will not keep anything from you that you need to know."

She frowned, clearly not loving his answer, but she eventually nodded. "I get it, but I can't do *this*—" she motioned to each of them "—if we can't be open. Well, *open-ish*. I know that your work requires certain amounts of limitations, but when it comes to here and our lives, I need to know everything about this case. And so you are aware, I wasn't judging you, AJ." Amber looked at him with a pleading expression.

"You absolutely were judging, Amber." He squeezed her hand like he was trying to make it okay. "And it's understandable that you would judge. I've done a lot of things I'm not proud of in my life. Yet, if we try to date, I'll never do anything to hurt you."

She gave him a gentle smile, like she heard the well-intentioned promise, one he couldn't keep. "Let me think about this—*us*."

He slipped his hand from hers. He wanted to tell her she could trust him. And that he really would do nothing to hurt her, and yet he knew from his many experiences on the battlefield when a battle was lost. He had been stupid for even thinking that he should approach the topic of being together. She could do better than a man like him. Besides, now she knew more about him than just about anyone, and he couldn't blame her for not wanting to be a part of any of it. If someone came at him with what he was trying to sell her, he would've run. In fact, he was surprised she was even still in the truck.

"And, hey, maybe it's better if we just don't do this, but… Yeah." He stared out the window, consumed by the awkwardness between them. Maybe this was part of the reason he didn't do relationships. He definitely wasn't good at talking about them.

"Did your sister say anything else about Tammy?" Amber asked, dispelling some of the awkward tension between them and changing the subject.

"She said that Tammy had been staying at the Red Lion."

"We could go see if she's there," Amber said, motioning in the direction of the hotel.

"I don't think it's a good idea for me to be seen anywhere close to Tammy's last known location. You know the detective would have a field day with that."

Amber's features tightened. "You know, if things go squirrely, the detective and his team are going to be watching that security footage at the hotel pretty closely." Amber tapped on the steering wheel, but she turned in the direction of the hotel downtown. "Then again, if it's not her out there in the woods, we'll have an answer whether she's alive if we go over there and knock on the door and she opens it."

He hadn't thought of it that way. If they were making this all into something it wasn't, they would look like fools. They needed to do a little recon—if nothing else, it would give them some peace of mind.

"Plus, thinking about this from the detective's point of view... As far as you telling me the truth about the ring, I think it's going to be helpful. Clearly, you're willing to work with law enforcement so it's not like you're concealing things. That being said, you definitely should tell the detective about the ring when you meet with him. He's probably going to ask you questions as to why you didn't give him the information earlier. So be prepared."

"If he starts asking any condemning questions, Kendra already made it clear that I'm to call her for representation."

"I have to say, from a law-enforcement standpoint, I hate when people lawyer up," Amber said. "However, from a civilian perspective, you're so lucky to have a lawyer as a sister, do you know that?"

"Oh, I'm more than aware. She has saved our asses for the last couple years now." He sighed. Brick buildings passed by as they made their way downtown. "My sister was actually shot once. She was the victim of domestic violence. Now she has started to make it her mission to help women who are in situations like where she once found herself. I'm really proud of her."

"As you should be. That is amazing." Amber shook her head slightly, like she was in disbelief.

"What?" he asked.

She stopped and let a man cross the street in front of them. "Is there anyone in your family who isn't just amazingly accomplished?" She laughed. "Seriously, the more you talk about them, the more intimidated I become."

"You weren't intimidated just by the fact that we were contractors?" he asked, with a laugh.

"Oh, for sure. I guess, though, knowing you were a contractor was fine, so long as your weapons weren't pointed at me."

He was strangely comforted. There were women who liked being with men who were in different areas of special operations and special forces, but finding women who were into what many looked at as mercenaries, or spies, was a little bit more of a challenge. Again, it came down to the unpredictable lifestyle. She seemed to understand that, though, and it only made him want her more. However, her being resistant to the idea of a relationship really was good for both of them.

She pulled to a stop a block down from the Red Lion, but within view of their parking lot.

"The SUV right there," he said pointing at a white Pathfinder. "That's her car."

Though he had known Tammy could be creeping back into his world, until now, he had been keeping some irrational hope that it was nothing more than his own imagination. Yet, seeing her car with the dent just above the left rear-wheel quarter panel, where Tammy had backed into a pole on their third date, and the scratch where she had opened the back into a trailer hitch... It brought everything she had been and all of the old feelings he'd packed away back into the light. Damn, if he didn't want to run away.

Chapter Twelve

Detective Baker could hardly be called intimidating. It wasn't that the man wasn't capable—AJ was damn sure that if he needed to be, the guy could make a grown-ass man piss himself, but for the most part, he just seemed nonchalant. Everything about him, from the way he leaned back in his chair and threw his arm over the one next to him when he laughed, to the way he seemed to constantly wear a low-grade smile, was almost *inviting*. That fact might have been what disarmed people and made the man good at his job.

"So, you think the ring may have belonged to your ex-fiancée?" Baker asked, his peg tooth shimmering thanks to the pendant lights hanging over the island in AJ's little cabin.

AJ liked how Baker carefully picked his words. They weren't incriminating or accusatory, just a statement of what may or may not have been the case.

"Yeah," AJ said, glancing at Amber, who was casually sitting beside Baker on one of the barstools.

Baker looked over at Amber and tapped his fingers on the top of the empty chair next to him. "And he told you about this ring this morning, without you prompting?"

Amber nodded.

There was a pregnant pause, as if Baker was trying to make heads or tails of the information they had given him.

"What kind of relationship did you and Tammy have?" Baker asked.

AJ thought for a long moment, but all he could think about was the moment they had said goodbye in person for the last time. It had been in Louisiana, while he had been overseeing contractors. She had come down to visit him and the entire weekend had been nothing but a hellacious fight. "Our relationship unraveled from the inside. I wasn't there when she needed me, and I couldn't be upset for her feeling that way."

"Were there a lot of hurt feelings...? Hers or yours?" Baker asked, but his body language shifted slightly, and he leaned in, tenting his fingers in front of him like he was listening intently and genuinely concerned.

AJ knew that game entirely too well; he had

taken his fair share of interrogation courses over the years, too. No matter what Baker came at him with, though, he felt comfortable in the knowledge that he had nothing to hide… at least when it came to his personal life.

"She initiated the breakup and seemed to move on with her life. That was two or three years ago." He looked over at Amber. "I also told her, Amber, all about this," he said, motioning to her with a smile before looking back at Baker. "I am happy to be an open book when it comes to everything to do with Tammy."

"Then why did you not tell me about the ring last night? Why did you wait?" Baker asked.

"Like I said, I was hoping I was wrong." He put his palms down on the island, the stone cold against his hot skin. He wanted to tell Baker that he also felt the need to protect STEALTH first, to follow the chain of command there in order to protect secrets that went back generations and crossed oceans. Everything happening here had the potential to open a veritable Pandora's box of issues. He had to be careful. "Hell, I may actually be wrong. I hope I am, but then I was told about Tammy being here in town, I knew the odds were stacked in favor of it being Tammy's ring."

"Did you see her while she was here in town?" Baker asked.

AJ shrugged. "Like I said, I only just found out she was here. After that, Amber and I ran over to the hotel and I did see her car."

"But you never saw Tammy today or any other time in the last few weeks?" Baker continued.

Amber's eyes were wide and she opened her mouth to speak, as though she wanted to say something in AJ's defense. He gave her a tiny shake of the head. He appreciated that she wanted to help him, but this was something he was going to have to handle.

"I have had nothing to do with her. She reached out a few times over the years since we broke up, but I didn't talk to her. You are welcome to look over my phone records, if you like."

Baker nodded. "I appreciate that."

"I've been really up front with you. Now I hope you're willing to be up front with me as well," AJ said, staring down Baker. "You called this meeting today. What were you hoping to learn? Or, was there something you wanted to tell me?"

The detective had a guilty smile. "You know, you and I make pretty damned good friends. I can see we speak the same language."

"You mean that we don't blow smoke?" AJ asked with a laugh. "You got that right. I've been at my game, and you've been at yours, for long enough that we don't have to dance around subjects."

Baker tilted back his head with a laugh, and the action made his paunch jiggle. He definitely had the body type of a detective. For a moment, AJ wondered if the gut was a requirement of the job, or if it just naturally came with the gig over time. As much as he judged the guy, he definitely understood how a person's job could both physically and emotionally change them.

"So, are you going to tell me why you called this meeting?"

Baker turned to Amber. "Miss Daniels, I appreciate you being here for this, but I would like to talk to AJ alone for a minute, if you wouldn't mind?" he asked, but there wasn't really a question as much as there was an order.

"Absolutely, I'll be outside." Amber got up from her seat, and as she moved AJ noticed the sweat around her vest.

She must have been feeling as nervous as him. It made him wonder why. He had been as honest with her as possible. Knowing what she did about him, it seemed like she should have been reassured that he would make it out of this line of questioning without too much of a problem. Maybe she saw something in him or in his demeanor that set off alarm bells, and if she saw it…then Baker definitely would.

He pinched the inside of his palm as he tried to control himself and his desire to start explaining all the ways he was innocent. Honest people reacted to interrogation in a variety of ways, but the most common was indignation, and another was candor. While he could act indignant that Baker was calling his life and actions into question, he would never sell outrage. He could understand why Baker was asking the questions he was, so pretending anything else would come off as false.

Amber put her hand on his shoulder and gave it a reassuring squeeze before walking out of the cabin. The door clicked shut behind her.

Baker watched behind him before turning back. "Amber is a great woman, good warden, but I don't want you not to be able to tell me something just because you are uncomfortable."

That was a damn good reason for him to ask her to step out, not to mention the fact he had made sure to validate her job performance.

No. I can't keep going down this maniacal tunnel of overthinking.

This was a terrible habit, but then it had saved his ass just as many times as it had been a hindrance.

"Like I said, here to help. Whatever you need to do to get what you need, I am happy to acquiesce." He put his hands up in supplication, a simple gesture but a powerful one.

"Much appreciated." Baker tapped his fingers together. "I actually came here because of a phone call I received."

AJ nodded, but all the questions rolled through his mind and forced him to pinch the skin of his palm harder. Instead of speaking up, he allowed Baker to run the show.

"Do you know if Tammy had a child or children?"

AJ felt the blood rush from his face. "No. None that I know of…why?"

"We did a search of Tammy's hotel room today. Apparently, your ex… Tammy had a child. A boy named Charlie. He is two years old. And, you were named as the boy's father on a notecard we found."

A stiff breeze could have knocked him over. He had a son. A boy he'd never known existed. He'd not even considered being a father before. Not really.

Wait—if they searched Tammy's hotel room in the first place, did that mean the cops had ID'd the hand?

He couldn't think straight.

Was he a father?

Holy crap...

He did the quick math in his head. If the baby was two, it was definitely possible that he could have been the boy's father, but he doubted Tammy wouldn't have told him. They hadn't hated each other that much, bad breakup aside.

In fact, he and Tammy had talked about having children on a few occasions, but their talks always dissipated once they started really delving into what the needs of a child would entail—who would be responsible for feeding and caring for the newborn baby around the clock? When they'd been together, he was gone more than he was home and all the burden had fallen on her. He hadn't blamed her for not wanting a family with him, and yet...

"Yeah, I don't think that can be true." AJ ran his hand over his face as if he could wipe away all the possibilities with the action. "You guys haven't found out anything about the remains, have you? Did you even find any more remains or was the hand the only part?"

"Slow down. Let's deal with one thing at a time." Baker stood up and walked to the sink. He grabbed a glass out of his cupboard and poured a glass of water, then handed it over to AJ. "Here, take a drink. I can tell this came as quite a shock for you."

AJ nodded in appreciation as he took the glass and took a long drink. Tammy had damn well never said a word about a kid. If she had, he would have done the right thing. He would have taken the kid into his life, been a father in every way that Tammy would have allowed him to be. Hell, he would have loved to have had a kid.

"So, back to my original line of questions, AJ. Did you and Tammy have an antagonistic relationship? One where she would have wanted to keep the existence of a child secret from you?"

He stiffened. "She didn't like the work my family does, and she knew I wouldn't be around a lot." AJ's voice threatened to give out as all the reasons he wouldn't have made a good father came rushing to the forefront of his mind.

Maybe she had just thought he wasn't up to the task.

That hurt more than learning about the boy.

"*Is* the child really mine?" He choked on the words as he spoke.

"To be clear, we are just trying to get as much information as possible." Baker sat back down in his chair, but there was an apologetic look upon his wide face. "As such, I wanted to talk to you before we pull out all the stops to find the child to see if you might possibly know where he would be located."

"I didn't even know I had a kid. How would I know where to find him?" AJ asked. "It's just…none of this makes any sense."

For the first time since their conversation had started, Baker didn't seem capable of looking him in the eye.

"What aren't you telling me?" AJ asked.

Baker jerked, his eyebrows rose and he looked slightly thrown that he had been caught in his attempt to suppress information. "You didn't have anything to do with Tammy's hand being found on your ranch, did you? Maybe so you could gain custody of your child without a long, drawn-out legal battle that could possibly put your family in the public eye?"

"What in the actual hell? Are you kidding me? What a load of…" He struggled to keep his temper under control. "This," he said, motioning between them, "is the first time I'm hearing about a kid. Mine, or otherwise." He pursed his lips, then let out his breath in an attempt to regain composure, when all he wanted to do was find out who would ever say such a thing about him. "And you are absolutely crazy if you think I'd intentionally hurt a woman I loved. We may not be together anymore, but that doesn't mean I just stopped caring about her."

Baker nodded. "From what I know about you and your family, I don't doubt what you are telling me. I'm satisfied that you didn't know about this boy or his mother. As for the hand…" The man looked down at his own as hands he opened and closed them into loose fists. "I had our forensics team pull the fingerprints."

There was that feeling again, the sensation of all the blood rushing from his body and pooling on the floor. In a moment of being irrational, he wondered if he stood up and walked away if he would actually leave bloody footprints in his wake.

"Was it her?" His question was simple, but those words held every hope and fear in his entire being.

"Unfortunately, it appears as though the hand *did* belong to her. We can't say for certain, but we believe she is likely deceased."

Just like that, what remained of his quaking resolve gave way and he dropped to his knees. It was one hell of a feeling to have his life unravel.

Chapter Thirteen

There had been very few times Amber could recall when she had heard a man sob. One was when her brother had passed away, and she had been there to hold her father's hand when the nurses shared the news. Her father had gone to pieces in a way that she had never before witnessed and never wanted to see again.

From inside the cabin, she could hear a noise like that of her father's and it made her heart threaten to shatter. She walked to the door and held the knob, not sure if she should go in and take care of AJ in his moment of need, or stay outside and be here for him in the moment of his choosing.

If he was anything like her stoic father, he would never want her to see him broken. AJ had shown her how strong he was from the moment she had first met him out in the timber. If she ran to him now, he would be just as likely to shirk from her touch as he was to fall into it.

She could only imagine what Baker had said to him behind these closed doors to make him fall to pieces like this, but she wanted to punch her fellow officer in the nose for hurting AJ.

Without realizing it, she had been gripping the handle so hard that her hand was shaking.

She couldn't do this. She couldn't stand out here in the cold when AJ so clearly needed her. Yet, if she went in there and took him in her arms like she wanted to, the nature of their relationship would definitely come into question. She had come here to do a job and was already too close to the man she had been working with—that kind of thing was taboo. Until now, she hadn't feared losing her job over it, but if she made it obvious, she very well could find herself in the HR office at the regional headquarters by the end of the week.

Still, that wasn't reason enough to stop her from going to him.

Without giving it another thought, she opened the door. Baker was standing beside AJ; his hand was on his shoulder, and when she walked in, Baker looked up. There was a pained expression on his face.

"What happened?"

"The hand…is Tammy's," AJ said, looking

up at her. He ran the back of his hand under his nose, which was running. There were tear streaks on his cheeks and the sight of him in such a state pulled at her heartstrings.

She nearly snarled at the detective. "Go grab him a Kleenex." She pointed in the direction of the bathroom.

The detective opened his mouth like he was going to argue, but after looking at her, he seemed to think better of it before doing as she said.

She moved to AJ's side. "Just because they gave us a positive ID on the hand, it doesn't mean she's dead."

"You and I both know she is dead." AJ pulled in a deep breath like he could regain his composure in a single inhale.

She put her hands on his shoulders and stared into his eyes. "You are going to be okay. No matter what happens, I'm here for you. We've got this."

"There might be a kid out there… *My kid.*" He choked on the words and tears started to well in his eyes. "Baker asked if I had anything to do with Tammy's possible death for custody reasons."

A chill skittered through her. *A child? A child* he hadn't thought to tell her about…who might be missing. Her fingers trembled as she pushed away a tear that had broken through his resolve. Her heart broke for him, but she didn't know what to say. There was nothing in anyone's life that could prepare a person for a moment like this. Not only had he just lost a woman who had once meant a great deal to him, but he might have also just lost a son.

A son he hadn't mentioned to her. Had he been lying to her and stringing her along this whole time?

She tried to tell herself he wouldn't do that to her, that he hadn't been using her and this was all just a misunderstanding, but she struggled.

She started to step away from him, but before she could, he reached up and held her in place.

"I didn't know I had a son. I had no idea. I still don't even know if it's true."

From behind her, Baker cleared his throat. "He is telling you the truth."

Turning to the detective, she couldn't help the sneer that registered on her lips. "Did you look into the allegations before you just hit him with this?" she snapped.

"As much as I could," Baker said, giving her a look of understanding and pity.

She hated that look. He had no right to completely overturn AJ's life in such a way without a positive ID. She was absolutely furious, and every word came out like a spent round, each narrowly missing her intended target as Baker never seemed to waiver. "You need to get out there, do the legwork. How dare you come here and break him like this?"

"Miss Daniels… Amber." Baker said her name like it was an apology. "I didn't come here to hurt him, or anyone for that matter. It is just an unfortunate part of my job that sometimes I have to be the bearer of some damn hard truths and even harder allegations." He didn't move any closer to her.

She appreciated that the man could tell that he was almost within striking range and knew to keep his distance. She wasn't sure that she could completely control her rage, no matter how much she understood that he wasn't the person she should be targeting and she was here as a guest out of professional courtesy. He was only the messenger and as much as she hated this, he was doing his job and asking the required questions to keep the public and the ranch safe.

No one had to like them, least of all *her*.

Just like that, she was pulled back to reality and it hit her harder than she could have expected. This wasn't her battle. No matter how much she cared about AJ, he could have been lying to everyone. He could have been playing her right now and she could have been acting like a fool for a man who was using her.

Yet, everything in her gut told her that this was real. That AJ was a broken man and not just putting on an act for her and Baker's benefit.

She pulled herself back from AJ. At the very least, she needed to talk to Baker alone. As much as she hated this, she and Baker were on the same team. "We need a word." She pushed past Baker as she motioned for him to follow her outside.

As he stepped outside, she slammed the door behind them. She walked out into the falling night to the middle of the road that led to the different cabins. Spinning around, she came face-to-face with the barrel-chested man. "Why didn't you notify me of your findings? I thought I was a part of this investigation."

The battle-hardened detective looked her in the eyes. "You are, but we both know that your capacity for this is limited. I know you are angry and you feel that I was working behind your back. But you need to be objective." He gave her arms a light, reassuring squeeze. "This situation is outside of your job requirements. I can tell that you and AJ Spade are something more than work colleagues, and I'd be remiss if I didn't tell you what a terrible idea I think that is. Yet, I don't think it's going to matter to you. Not with you looking at me like you are."

Some of the anger seemed to seep out of her as the man's words struck her like a fist to the gut. Amber wasn't sure what had made her think that confronting the detective was a good idea, but she felt like a mama bear going straight to rage and attack when it came to protecting her cubs. AJ definitely wasn't her cub, yet she couldn't help the instinct to protect him…even from a bear who was professionally far larger and more powerful than herself.

At least Baker was kind in his rebuff of her charge. However, just because he'd spoken to her like this, it didn't assuage her anger, at least not completely.

"You… This… You should have told me," she said, trying to gain control over her words as feebly as she could gain control over her feelings. "I was the first officer on the case, after all." And how dare he blindside AJ with this information? They could've broken it to him together.

Baker cupped her shoulder like he must have done every time he delivered bad news and the motion reminded her of her father the day her brother died. She hated the feeling and the memories it sparked.

"I couldn't tell you, or anyone else, until I went in there and got a good read on him. I needed to know he wasn't the one pulling the strings here."

She exhaled, hard. "And? What did you get?" Every cell of her being silently prayed that Baker had come to the same conclusions about AJ and his integrity as she had.

Baker's brow furrowed, as though he was trying to attempt to reconcile his thoughts and his feelings. "I think AJ is a good man. He tries to do the right thing and his heart is in the right place. Yet, that doesn't mean he isn't guilty of wrongdoing here, Amber."

Until now, she hadn't realized she was crying, but hot tears rolled down her cheeks like the punches she wanted to throw. She shook her head, as if she could shake away the truth of what he'd just said.

"Don't misunderstand me." Baker gripped her hand, hard. "I don't think AJ killed Tammy. My gut is saying he isn't behind this. He wouldn't be stupid enough to leave a trail."

"Did he know about the boy?" she asked.

Baker shook his head. "There's no way. I think what really broke him was when I told him about the note Tammy had left behind, saying he was the father. He had no idea that Charlie existed—and as for the allegations that he might have killed her. *Never.*"

She exhaled and her grip loosened on the detective.

"Amber, as a fellow law enforcement officer, I'm asking you to help out on this case. We need to find out if this boy is dead or alive. If not, AJ may see jail time for this."

From behind Detective Baker, AJ walked outside. Up the road, by the main house, there was the sound of truck engine revving to life.

Dollars to donuts, AJ had called Zoey. He could see her through the front window the closer the vehicle got. Hell, his whole entire family was probably already in the know… and they were all coming to his side, ready to find the missing child.

It was one hell of a family and team that would come to the aid of their brother and teammate like this when he needed them all the most. She would give almost anything to be a part of a world like this—a world in which a family stood together.

The truck pulled to a stop beside them and Zoey came out with two other men that Amber recognized as Mike and Troy, AJ's brothers.

"What in the hell is going on?" Zoey charged toward the detective. "Did you talk to Kendra?"

Zoey looked over at AJ, who was standing on the edge of the porch, a stunned expression on his face. "AJ, did you call Kendra?"

He nodded.

"Good," Zoey said, turning back to Baker. "You're a friend of ours, yes?"

Baker nodded, and for the first time since she had known the man, he looked slightly afraid.

"I don't want you to do a damned thing, or call a single person, until we get more info about this boy. Do you understand?" Zoey stared down the detective like he was a disobedient child and not the only person who stood between AJ being arrested or being cleared of any wrongdoing.

Baker nodded. "You know I have a job to do here, too."

Amber stepped back from Baker and let Zoey move closer. "And what do you think that job is, right now?" Zoey growled. "Tammy is dead."

"Is she?" Baker asked, sounding like he had just found a little store of bravery.

"Only you would know that, Baker, but we all know that this now needs to be treated like a possible crime scene."

Baker nodded. "Yes."

"We won't stand in your way. We want to

get to the bottom of Tammy's *possible death.* We are going to work with you, and do everything—and I mean *everything*—to get answers. Yes?" Zoey asked, leading him to the answers by his nose.

Baker nodded.

"Give us twenty-four hours to get to the bottom of this, and then you can have this all back. Do we have a deal?"

"Zoey, you know I can't do that," Baker said.

"Why can't you? First, we don't even know if she is alive or dead. Seems like there is no actual crime to speak of—that being said, you can keep your men out here on the ranch, but I want you to go inactive for the time." When Baker started shaking his head, she gave him an imploring look. "Please. You know we have the team and resources to do this, and if this boy is one of ours—" she glanced at AJ "—then we're not going to sit back and do nothing. We can help you. Whatever we find, we will give you. All I'm asking is that you get out of the way and let us do what we do best. In return, everyone will get the answers they need…and justice will be done."

Chapter Fourteen

AJ knew all too well how quickly a life could change—a car accident, a diagnosis, a proposal or even a phone call. He had been on the end of far too many life-changing moments, both receiving and giving. Yet they all paled in comparison to the secret the detective had shared—AJ was likely a father.

Not only had he been thrust into a new life, a new definition of himself, but he was also forced to face the fact that his baby was also at risk. In his wildest imaginings, he would have never gotten to this point. This was worse than a nightmare—at least in nightmares, a person could wake up.

Until now, he hadn't hated Tammy. He had moments when he'd disliked her, and he had been relieved that she was no longer a part of his life, but now a sense of loathing filled him. This secret—or rather, this *lie*—didn't just affect her, or even himself. Her not telling him about the child had also hurt the baby.

He thought of all of his nieces and nephews, now more than five of them, who would have loved to meet Charlie and incorporate him into their life here on the ranch. Tammy had denied him that. She'd denied his entire family the chance to meet one of their own.

"AJ?" Amber asked, her voice gentle and supplicating, as though she could sense the war within him and feared catching a stray round.

"Hmm?" Words failed him.

Since she had come to his rescue with the detective, he had been barely able to speak. Thankfully, she seemed to understand that he had reverted back to a guttural, instinctive language—it was the dialect of a pain so severe it could only be called transformative agony.

"Zoey wants to talk to you in her office. Do you think you are up to going in there?"

He hated that he had been brought to his knees, but nothing in his life had prepared him for a moment like this—a moment that went far beyond betrayal.

Amber held out her hand and he put his fingers in hers. He stood up from the couch. The fire in the fireplace was crackling and it was emitting tongues of light that lashed over the floor like they were reaching for him and wanting to consume what little was left.

He couldn't give in to his pain. He couldn't. It had been more than half a day now. Sleep had been impossible, but luckily Amber had drifted into a slumber in his arms and had gotten some rest. Even in what could have been a peaceful moment, all he had found himself thinking about was all the nights he had lost in his son's life, nights when the baby had been down with a cold or an ear infection. Nights when he should have been holding him in his arms.

He followed Amber blindly, thinking only of how he was going to get to his son.

He swallowed back the lump in his throat that seemed to rise every time he thought about making it to the toddler, only to find out it was too late.

Amber knocked on the office door, and they made their way inside. The room hadn't really changed much since he had been in it the other day, and yet he felt as though he was in another world. Even the pictures on the screens seemed to take on a different, more ominous feel.

Zoey looked at him and then pulled out a chair and motioned for him to sit down, like he was some kind of invalid. His boss wasn't the kind to feel sorry for anyone, and she certainly wasn't the kind to take it easy on a person, so the look of pity on her face when she glanced at him threatened to shred what little resolve he had left.

Damn it. He wasn't this man.

He didn't get dropped to his knees like this.

Still, here he was.

"Amber told me about the notecard. I tried to get a copy of it from Baker, but it's a no-go for right now as this is a possible criminal investigation. Regardless, it's going to be okay," Zoey said as he took a seat.

Amber moved beside him like she was guarding him against any further pain—if only she could have. If only life took pity on those it inhabited, but it was a cruel master. Still, he appreciated it. Once again, she was proving to be a comfort to him when he needed it most.

"Find anything?" he asked, his voice hoarse and raspy.

Zoey sent him an odd, kind smile that didn't seem to fit her face. No one was being themselves and it was all because of him. He hated this.

He cleared his throat. It had been a long night and he had given himself to the feelings that coursed through him—now he needed to keep moving forward. It was the time for work.

"We managed to find a record of Charlie." Zoey motioned toward the computer screen at the center of her work area. There, on the screen, was a picture of a baby. It looked as though it had been pulled from a hospital's birth announcement page. "His birthday is April twenty-seventh. There was no paternity test and no father named on the birth certificate, but from what we know, he could definitely be yours."

He stared at the boy's chubby cheeks. The blond baby was sucking on his fist and gazing up with unfocused blue eyes. AJ never thought newborn babies were cute, but this little one was different than most he had seen. He was plump and round instead of the nearly translucent hairy creatures that cried any time he was near.

He also never thought newborn babies looked like one parent or the other, but as he looked at the infant, he could make out the almond-shaped eyes that often went hand in hand with the people of his family.

There was no question. This little being was his. AJ could just feel it…and just like he could feel the boy's life force, or whatever it was that he intrinsically picked up on, he also already loved him.

"Charlie," he said, putting his hands on

the edge of the computer screen as though he could reach through the screen and touch the baby's soft skin.

"Charles Alexander Reynolds," Zoey said, touching his arm gently as she said his given first name. "You and Tammy may have had your problems, but she gave him your first name as his middle one."

Amber smiled over at him. "Your name is Alexander?"

He nodded as he dropped his hand from the screen and turned toward her. "Yeah, Alexander James. My family has just always called me AJ." He looked back at the baby on the screen. "I know this is crazy, Zoey, but would you mind printing me that picture?"

She sat down at her computer and a second later, there was the sound of a printer.

Amber slipped her hand into his and gave it a squeeze. "Are you okay?" she asked, putting her head against his shoulder.

"I will be, when we find him." He reached up and gave her a gentle hug.

Zoey grabbed the picture from the printer and handed it to him.

Taking it, he stared down at the little cherubic face. This was his baby, and in a way, this was the first time he was actually touching him. Emotions pooled within him and tears welled in his eyes, threatening to spill once again.

He hated that he cried. It absolutely floored him that within hours he had gone from a man who could unleash hell on his enemies to a man weeping over a baby.

Thankfully, Amber didn't seem to judge him poorly. She really was too good for him.

"We are going to age him up, and then run a facial-recognition program and see if we can pull anything about his location online. From there, we are going to go through all of Tammy's information and contact what few family members she has left. So far, we've found her social-media locations and run a geofence based on her phone's last known locations." Zoey picked up a piece of paper from the desk by her keyboard. "We came up with these coordinates."

There was a series of numbers on the paper she handed him.

"Her phone went dark four days ago. I'm thinking that gives us a window of a few days for when she went missing."

"Do you have any indication that Charlie was with her at that time?" His mind went to the predator that had set this all into motion. If Tammy had been killed by the griz...

A bear would usually go after the more vulnerable prey. A two-year-old would definitely not put up a fight.

The thought made him sick to his stomach.

Amber squeezed his arm and took the piece of paper with the coordinates. "We will look into these, but first we need to go out and check on our trap."

He pulled his arm out of her grasp. Though he shouldn't have been irritated that a bear would take precedence, he couldn't help his irritation. "Who cares about the damned bear?" He shouldn't have been rubbed wrong by her words but he couldn't help it. "Screw the bear. I have a kid to worry about."

She stepped back from him and her face fell, along with her shoulders. "I… Why don't you just stay here? I can run out there and then you can use this time to help Zoey." She flashed a look at Zoey.

He had hurt her. "Amber…" He groaned. "I'm sorry. I didn't mean it like that. I just…"

She shook her head as she peered at the floor. "You're fine. The bear is my job, anyway."

He reached for her, but she gently pulled away.

As she turned away, he thought he saw pain in her expression. He was such an ass. She had come here to help him and his family, and now he was sniping at her. From the second she had stepped foot on the ranch, all she'd done had been for him. He'd had no right to lose his patience with her, even if he was struggling.

Zoey tipped her head in Amber's direction and motioned for him to go after her, but he shook his head. He needed to be here, in the office, where the magic happened in finding his son. As though Zoey could read his thoughts, she mouthed, *It's fine. Go.*

He shook his head. He wanted to be with Amber—that wasn't a question—but somewhere out there was a little boy who might need him even more.

Walking over, Zoey pushed him toward the door leading outside. "Amber, wait!" she called after her.

Amber stopped as she made her way to her pickup. "You coming?" she asked Zoey.

She shook her head. "AJ is. He'll be right out."

"Damn it, Zoey," he whispered so only she could hear. "I need to help find Charlie."

"You aren't going to be able to do anything in this office that I can't. Plus, I have our whole tech crew working from around the world. Just go apologize and try to clear your head out there. If you don't, you will regret it."

There were a million moments he regretted in his life, but he was glad that his boss was helping him from regretting this one. Amber was special; there was no denying that. No matter what he did here, though, he couldn't help the nagging feeling in his gut that he was doing the wrong thing and making the wrong choice.

Zoey pushed him outside. "We've got this. Trust your team. Just go look into the pins and let me know if you find anything. In the meantime, know that there is no stone that our team will leave unturned."

Though he wanted to find peace in Zoey's words, he found only confusion. She had no right to turn him away when it came to his role in finding his son, but then she was his boss—so she did.

He exhaled, his breath making a cloud of visible emotions in the cold night. Every bit of that mist was a demon that he was fighting. Unfortunately, no matter how much he tried, he would never be done fighting within himself.

Amber was waiting for him inside the truck when he got in. She was silent as she put the truck in Drive and they bumped down the snowy road, which was now so well-traveled that there were deep ruts filled with icy potholes that were shattered and left jagged by tires.

"I am sorry about losing my temper back

there," he said. "That's not like me." *But nothing about this situation is normal.*

Amber sent him a soft smile. "I know you're going through a lot. I can only imagine all of the things you must be thinking and feeling." She hesitated for a moment before she continued. "And I realize that you don't need me bringing any more stress to your life. So as soon as we are done, I think I should head out."

That was the last thing he wanted. He wanted her to stand by his side and tell him everything was going to be okay, and that they were going to find his son and the boy would be healthy and safe. It was unexplainable, but he felt letting her go from the ranch would be letting her go from his life, and he wasn't ready to say goodbye just yet.

Surprisingly, as they drove to the area where they had set the bear trap, it appeared that no one else was in the area. Detective Baker had pulled out his entire team. The man really must have had the utmost faith that he was innocent. AJ appreciated it.

Baker really did have his back. It felt good knowing that the detective was a man of his word. Now he just hoped that they didn't let him down.

In the distance, in the trees, the bear trap was obscured in the shadows. From where they had parked, he couldn't tell whether or not the trap had been sprung, but from the tense look on Amber's face, he grew concerned.

She turned off the pickup and stepped out, but as she did, he noticed her putting her hand to her sidearm, instinctually. He followed suit, reaching down to his ankle holster, and pulled out his Glock, before stepping out of the truck.

"Is everything okay?" he asked, moving to her side.

She nudged her chin in the direction of the trap. "Houston, I think we have a bear."

He'd never been one to be afraid of wild animals, but the thought of walking up on a bear seemed like it was against his better judgment. "Do we need to call in your team?"

"If this is the collared bear we are after, we're going to have to make some phone calls. We need to find out if it is your bear first, then we can work on getting it released in a different location. That is, if it's not a *known* nuisance bear."

"You okay releasing this bear if it had something to do with Tammy's death?"

Amber stopped moving, and looked him dead in the eyes. "Without knowing the circumstances of Tammy's potential death, this is going to be tough." Her hand dropped from her gun, and she seemed to have taken pause. "We have two options. We can euthanize the bear, and do an analysis of its stomach contents… But even that wouldn't tell us if the bear was responsible in her death or if it was merely scavenging. Or, we can simply treat the bear like a nontroublesome animal and relocate it."

The answer seemed obvious to him. There was no sense in euthanizing a bear that may or may not have had some impact on Tammy's death. If the bear was simply doing what bears do, and scavenging on the remains, it didn't seem right to penalize the animal.

"Before we make any choices," Amber said, "let's just get up there and make sure we even have a bear inside."

The trees around them whined and moaned as they slowly made their way to the steel culvert trap. The world around them was eerily quiet, and even though they were walking in the tracks left by her truck, their shoes squeaked on the cold snow. This morning's temperatures were brutally cold.

It was a little bit of a surprise that with this level of cold, a bear would have been out of its den. He'd always been taught as a kid that bears hibernated. As such, he would've thought they were sleeping nonstop through the winter.

"Is it normal for bears to be this quiet, when

they're trapped?" His breath made the familiar white cloud in the air as he spoke.

She shook her head. "Did I show you my scar, the one on my leg?"

"No. What happened?"

"A few months ago, I was helping my team do research with a grizzly bear. The big boar was so strong that he was capable of actually bending some of the steel bars. That was unbeknownst to me, until I was standing in front of the trap, and he reached through and managed to get a hold of my leg with his paw. Bears are a lot stronger and faster than anyone realizes, until they are on top of you."

She lifted up the leg of her pants, and there were four dark purple claw marks.

"Damn, that's one hell of a war wound. You should be showing that one off."

"I always kinda hide it. While it's a great bar story, it seems counterintuitive to tell anyone about an injury from a bear when I should know what I'm doing." She laughed as she spoke. "Though, I guess bringing that up right now, that's a bad idea, too."

He chuckled. For the first time since yesterday, he realized he had actually laughed. With it came a sense of relief. "I have no doubt about your professionalism or your abilities when it comes to handling wildlife."

She shot him a look. "Oh, I've been questioning it plenty, even without you doing so."

"Why would you do that?" he asked.

"Really?" The way she said it made it sound like he was missing something completely obvious, but he wasn't sure what she was implying. "It was not a great idea for me to kiss you." A faint blush rose in her cheeks.

Until now, he wouldn't have thought it possible, but it made her more beautiful. She quickly looked away and moved down the leg of her pants, covering her scar.

"We are both adults, there was nothing ethically questionable about kissing." He followed as she started to walk again. "As team leader, I wouldn't condemn one of my team members if they had been in a position like we are."

"You don't really expect me to believe that, do you?"

"Yeah, I do. I absolutely would not reprimand one of my team members. Not for a relationship. Now, if it somehow impacted their judgment, or affected their work, that would be different. But this thing with us…"

"You can't say that it's not affecting my job." She sounded at odds with herself.

"The only way this has affected your job is positively. At least, as far as I can tell. You're here on the ranch, you've been doing your job to the best of your ability—if anything, you've been more accessible. If I was your boss, I wouldn't even blink."

"I know you're trying to make me feel better, but you aren't going to sell me on this." She let out a resigned sigh.

This woman was so stubborn. Even when he made a sound argument, she was never going to let him change her opinion. He liked that about her—even if he wished he could make her see things from his perspective in order to keep her from feeling any undue pain.

There were no sounds coming from within the trap as they grew closer. Amber frowned. "Sometimes these things spring and we get nothing," she said, sounding slightly annoyed.

As they got nearer, though, on the snow leading up to the cage, there were the unmistakable tracks made by a grizzly's paw.

Stepping around the trap so he could look inside, there, lying behind the steel bars, he saw an enormous, motionless brown bear. Even from where he stood, he could tell the animal was dead.

Chapter Fifteen

Amber stared at the bear's remains. This was the last thing she had expected to find and the sight made her heart break. She loved all animals, yet this was a part of her job. Souls passed by her, the grim reaper.

Now it was up to her to find out how the bear had died…and why.

It seemed strange to her that this bear had made it all the way into the steel trap if it had been sick or injured. The griz couldn't have been inside long enough to have died of exertion or stress, either. In all of her days, this was the first time this kind of thing had ever happened.

Just to make sure the animal was deceased, she poked a stick through the steel bars and prodded the bear. It didn't move and there was no steady rise and fall of its chest. Its paws were stiff, nearly frozen from the cold.

"What do you think happened?" AJ asked. He looked at her with wide eyes, confused.

She shrugged. "No one was out here last night, were they?"

AJ shook his head. "I don't think so."

Amber hated the idea that someone on the ranch had something to do with this, and until they looked over the bear, she didn't want to jump to any conclusions.

She moved to the winch, which ran the lift for the gate, and pushed the button, then the steel trap door slowly lifted with a shrill whine of metal on metal.

Part of her expected the bear to jump up and charge at her as she stepped back. Yet, it remained motionless. The scar on her leg throbbed as she stepped closer to the bear, as though her body was reacting to the old trauma and warning her to stay back.

Kneeling down, her hands were shaking as she reached in and touched the bear. It was cool to the touch and definitely not going anywhere. Its head was resting just below the bait and if she hadn't been sure otherwise, it could appear to be just taking a winter slumber.

She touched the bear's back paw. It was enormous in comparison to the size of her hand. The claws alone were longer than her fingers. The power this animal had, what it conveyed, and the role it played in nature were incredible. Feeling an ethereal pull, she said a silent thank-you to the animal in honor of its life.

"Amber? Are you okay?" AJ asked.

She looked over her shoulder at him. "Yeah, I always give honor to animals when they have passed."

"That's really cool. I do the same when I have to, but it's been a long time," he said. He stepped up beside her, closed his eyes and did the same.

Moving deeper into the trap, now that she was sure she wasn't in immediate danger, she pulled back the bear's lip. The animal's teeth were short and the right canine was worn down completely to the gums. Touching the animal, she could feel its ribs.

"Is there anything in there, in the trap, that you know…belonged to Charlie?" AJ asked, his voice barely above a whisper.

She looked over her shoulder at him. "No. And from everything I've seen so far, I don't feel like this bear had any contact with him," she lied, trying to reassure the stressed man but aware that there was no way she could be sure without further analysis.

AJ nodded, seeming to find peace in her answer.

She glanced back at the bear. The animal was in poor body condition, especially considering how late it was in the season. Its fur was the same tawny brown of the hair they'd found wedged into the barbed wire on the fence, but until they got the DNA results, she couldn't be 100-percent certain this was the only bear they were dealing with.

"Do you want to grab me my bag out of the pickup? The one in the back seat. It has all my supplies in it for taking samples."

AJ nodded. "Yeah, do you need anything else?"

"Grab my phone. I'm going to need to get some pictures as well." She could hear his footfalls as he made his way out toward the pickup.

It was nice having another set of hands around when she was working. Normally, when she first arrived at a location she was on her own until the bear team got there to do their work before releasing an animal. As it was, with this being a deceased animal, it was all going to be on her shoulders. Unfortunately, as this bear was likely involved with Tammy's case, it meant that she was going to have to take it to the university.

She peeled back the front of the animal's lip. Inside was a tattoo. It was number 832, the female who had been feasting on chickens years back and had been relocated north. At twenty-nine, the griz was considered an anomaly for a wild bear. Normally they died well before the age of twenty-five and most before they were even a year old.

On the lips, around the tattoo and along the gums was an odd red rash. Its edges had started to turn black, almost necrotic. Yet, it didn't make sense. The bear hadn't been down long enough for any sort of decomp to start. She had to have been sick.

Amber ran her hand down the bear's torso, feeling for any sort of bullet wound or trauma, but found nothing but a thin bony figure. Even its hair wasn't as thick or oily and heavy as she normally saw in bears this time of year.

Without a doubt, this girl had been incredibly sick.

The bait had been taken down and some of it had been eaten. There was a sense of peace in knowing the animal had feasted before it had lost its battle against nature.

Many times, if humans were attacked by a bear, it was a bear in this physically deteriorated state, or one with cubs they were attempting to protect. In this case, it seemed possible that Tammy might have just been in the wrong place at the wrong time—

AJ came back as she stared down at the bear

and he handed her the phone. She snapped a few pictures, then with AJ's help, they turned over the bear and she took some of the other side. Amber pulled back the lips and got some pictures of the animal's teeth and the black marks on the gums. Even the tongue had some of the blackness. It was so strange, and it made her wonder if the bear had come in contact with some kind of toxin.

A few years back, a herd of elk had mysteriously died a few hundred miles from where they stood. After a long battery of tests, they had found out that because of a lack of food, the elk had resorted to feeding off lichens and mosses on a rock outcrop. The lichens had ended up being poisonous and the entire herd had perished. Perhaps something like that had happened here.

"What is going on with its mouth?" AJ asked, pointing at it.

She shrugged. "I don't know. I can't say I've ever seen anything like that before."

"Huh," he said, tapping his fingers on the steel of the trap. "You know what that reminds me of?"

She looked back at him, unsure of where he was going to go with his statement.

He had a serious expression. "You know…

Tammy's hand had that same weird blackness. Do you think they could have been related?"

"I can't imagine how, but without running tests I don't know." She shrugged as she tried to remember exactly what the hand had looked like—instantly she was brought back to the purple fingertips. "I mean... I thought the hand was just frostbitten, but I'd have to look at it closer. Even then, I'm not a medical examiner." With the elk, it took a good month to get the results back from all the labs they drew on.

There was a sound of a car approaching in the distance. "I hope you don't mind. I called my crew in case we needed more hands loading or unloading."

She smiled. "You and your family and friends make one hell of a team. You are a lucky man to have such an incredible support system." As she spoke, it hit her how alone she normally was, and it made her miss her brother more than ever. She would give anything to have him back. So much had been taken from their family when he had died.

"I really am a lucky man, but everything I have has taken a long time and a lot of work to accumulate—even the relationships with my family sometimes take a lot."

He had opened up, and everything she'd learned about him just made her more drawn to him. But after spending time with him and his family she wasn't entirely sure how well she would fit. This team was nearly seamless; they communicated and they adapted for one another. She wasn't even sure she would know where to start when it came to becoming a part of this team.

Not that what she and AJ had going could really be considered a team... Though, at the same time, that was exactly what it was. They were working together.

Going into her bag, she pulled out a set of nitrile gloves, tweezers and her sample collection kits. Moving around the bear, she carefully took hair, a tooth and tissue. Wrapping up with her collections, she looked up to realize that AJ and his two brothers were standing outside the culvert trap and watching her.

"That is seriously cool," Mike said, motioning toward the bear. "Can I touch it?" As he spoke, he looked a bit like a kid the night before his birthday party—all hope and smiles.

"Come on up," she said, motioning for him to step inside and check out the animal.

She explained the body state and showed him the lips, as she had done with AJ. Both of his brothers took turns checking it out. After a few minutes, her legs started to cramp and she made her way out of the trap.

Stretching, she stood beside AJ. "Thanks for that," he said, motioning to his brothers. "They love this kind of thing."

She nodded and for a second it felt like she'd known AJ for years.

Everything with AJ was confusing, though also not. It was simple. She loved to be around him. It was easy to talk to him and open up and tell him what she was thinking about things and why; and she couldn't say that she had ever had friends or romantic interests before where things had flowed so naturally.

Maybe it was that they were just cut from the same cloth. Or maybe they had just formed some empathic bond because of everything they had both been forced to face from the moment they had first met. There was definitely something to the idea of trauma bonding people. And yet, that wasn't what it felt like when she was close to him. When she was near him, she wanted to touch him and to hear him speak. It was simple, and it wasn't. She was afraid, and yet it was a *yearning*.

It was those feelings that actually scared her the most. She could put up with a lot and had seen many things that other people wouldn't and couldn't emotionally handle, but feeling safe and wanting to be near a man was where she apparently drew a line in the sand. It was almost funny in its absurdity.

"Hey, Amber," Troy said from inside the trap, his voice echoing off the steel and amplifying the sound. "If you want, Mike and I can run the animal to the lab for you."

She pulled off her gloves and shoved them into her pack with the samples she had taken for her work. "Actually, I was going to run it down to the university and their lab. They are doing the DNA testing, and—" She paused. "However, if you guys are offering, it would save me a drive. I could just let them know you're coming."

She wasn't exactly sure why she had given the go-ahead on this. Normally, she didn't mind all the windshield time. Admittedly, it probably had something to do with the oh-so-handsome man at her side. If she ran back into the city with the bear, those were hours that she wouldn't be able to help him. They still needed to check out the coordinates that Zoey had listed for them.

Sure, AJ was capable of going through GPS coordinates and running to the locations, but she didn't like the idea of him going to them alone. Even that was silly. He was literally a trained killer and she was worried about him. She huffed. If they ever actually had a real relationship, one that didn't leave her with ethical and moral conundrums, she doubted that she would ever stop worrying about him...regardless of his training.

"Are you sure you guys are okay with that? I know you are working your butts off with Zoey." *And the search for Charlie.* But she didn't dare say the last bit aloud.

"We're waiting on some phone calls and emails," Mike said, giving Troy a questioning glance.

Troy nodded. "Yep. We've got this. Why don't you guys just go ahead."

"I'll let the lab know you two are coming," she confirmed. "I'm sure they can meet you outside the Skaggs Building and get you all set up. Normally they have me pull into the underground area so anyone passing by doesn't get upset."

Troy nodded. "Got it. Shouldn't take us too long. Do you think you're going to need the trap set up again?"

"No. I think this is our girl." From here, she would just need to find out if this bear was Tammy's killer, but that was going to take some time and she was glad she wasn't the one who was going to have to get her hands dirty in finding out by doing the necropsy.

AJ stared at the bear and she was forced to

wonder if he was thinking the same things she was, and facing the same questions. "Are you okay, AJ?"

He jerked slightly as if she had pulled him out of some kind of daze. "Yeah, I'm sure I'll be fine. I'm just…" He waved his hands and appeared to struggle to find exactly the right word to explain the chaos that was likely happening inside his head and his heart.

"I'm sure you're exhausted." She grabbed her bag, then looped her arm through his and led him slowly back toward her truck. "Let's go check on these locations to see if we can find anything. Then you need to take a break. Hell, if you want, you can sleep while I drive. Fair?"

"I couldn't sleep now, not even if I tried. We need to find my son." He sent her a tired smile. "Amber, I hope you know how much your help means to me."

She laughed, dismissing his compliment gently. "That is just your exhaustion talking. Clearly, you're not at the top of your game." As she spoke, she found her feelings and her words at odds. She loved that he had expressed his gratitude and saw her in the manner in which she hoped he would— as a resource and a steady presence in his life, while being a person who wholeheartedly wanted the best for him—whether or not that meant she was going to have a place in his life.

For now, all they had was hope.

Chapter Sixteen

There were few other times he could remember feeling this exhausted. Once, while he had been going through his early training, his instructors had kept him and his class up for four days straight. By the end of the fourth day, he had started to hallucinate and he felt outside of his body. While that exhausted, the instructors had had them running and pushing their bodies past the point he thought he was physically able to continue.

It was during those weeks and months of work and training that he had found out exactly how tough he was. And yet, a little boy and a new friend were having the power to weaken him.

AJ didn't know exactly what it was in Amber that he saw; there were so many things that she was doing for him. Better, her actions and her words were matching. She wasn't just throwing him empty promises and pity. Instead she was knee-deep in the mire that was his life and the mystery that it was revolving around.

She really was an amazing woman. To make it all worse, at least when it came to his heart and his ever-growing feelings about her, she didn't want a relationship with him.

Add a child to the mix, and there was zero chance that she was going to change her mind. He didn't blame her for her choice before the news, and now he was glad she had chosen as she had. Regardless, it wasn't like he could have made a relationship work. Not now, not with so much on his plate and hanging in the balance.

He was just damn lucky he hadn't been arrested—they had probable cause, not to mention his withholding information.

His phone pinged with a message from Troy. They had loaded the bear into the back of one of the trucks from the ranch and were just about to head out to the lab.

He'd been thinking a lot about the bear, too. He had really assumed that the bear had been sleeping when they had first come upon her, but it hadn't taken long to prove otherwise. Though he felt bad for the loss, all he had been able to think about was what this animal— this enormous ball of fur, teeth and claws—

could have possibly meant for Tammy in her last moments.

From the way Amber had spoken, it was very likely that the animal had been behind his ex-fiancée's demise. Whether it had or it hadn't, he was still left with the nagging question of where Charlie was.

While the feeling in his gut couldn't tell him exactly what had happened to Tammy, there was no question about how it felt when it came to Charlie being his child. There was just some inexplicable link. Charlie was *his*.

He closed his eyes for a moment, blocking out the moon as it reflected off the snow and into the truck as Amber followed the robotic voice of their navigation system. According to the GPS coordinates and the nav system, they were heading to the Kootenai Falls Trailhead and parking area.

From the information he had so far gleaned from Zoey, Tammy's phone had pinged at that location for nearly a day. He wasn't sure what they were going to find. From the location alone, he could assume that Tammy had merely gone to the area to hike and perhaps camp. Nothing out of the ordinary, except for the fact it had been cold for the last two weeks—and according to the time line it would have only been in the low teens the night she had been at the trailhead.

Yet, it was something. It was a starting point in the search for Charlie.

That was...if Charlie was still alive.

He blanched at the thought.

The trailhead was not far from the ranch, and as they pulled into the parking area, he noted that if a person had a high-end spotting scope, it was possible to watch the entrance of the ranch's property.

Strange.

Amber was working on her phone as he got out and made his way around the trailhead. Based on the tracks, several cars had come and gone over the last few days, but there was no one in the parking lot. From the trailhead, there was a broken path in the snow, even one track that looked as though it had been made by a snowshoe. Everything about the area, except the view of the ranch's turnoff from the highway and entrance, seemed painfully routine.

As he came back to the truck, Amber looked up at him as he got in and buckled. "Did you find anything interesting?"

He shook his head, trying to ignore the feeling of failure that was creeping through his gut. This had been a waste of time. They were no closer to answers and no closer to finding Charlie.

"I have been looking over the maps and punching in the coordinates that Zoey gave us." Amber looked at her phone so he could see the pins that she had created on her mapping app. "Did you notice that every point is pretty close to the ranch?"

"Can I see your phone for a second?"

Without a moment of hesitation, she handed him her phone. He scrolled through the pins. There were a few other hiking trails that Tammy had stopped at. And two of the pins were just locations along logging roads, adjacent to the ranch and on US Forest Service land.

For someone from Montana, spending a couple weeks cruising around on logging roads and public land wasn't that unusual in the fall. That time of year, people spent a great deal of time hunting and exploring the woods.

"Zoey said these pins are from the last two or three weeks, but I wonder how long Tammy had been in Montana. I'll need to ask Zoey if she pulled any other info from the hotel." It wasn't a question, so much as a statement. It was this continued lack of information that was driving him bonkers. However, there was a lot of legwork to do, and not a lot of time to do it.

"Yeah," Amber said, like she could read his mind. "I would be happy just to know why she was here. I would've thought she would've tried to contact you quite a bit more, if her being here had something to do with you or your family. Yet, you said she was relatively quiet."

He picked up his phone and flipped through his call log, searching until he pulled up Tammy's call records. "Yeah, according to this, her last call to me was three months ago. She didn't even leave a message."

His thoughts moved to Tammy's phone. Cellphone records, at least for the company that she had been using, were only available for thirty days. That was, unless a law-enforcement agency filed for the company to retain records. As far as tracking her through those, it would be a challenge. They might be able to see whom she had been calling, but he was sure Zoey was already working on that angle.

Though Zoey could do quite a bit on the computer, especially along with their tech teams, they were limited by the resources available to them from cellular data. However, as he was pondering ways to track Tammy, his thoughts moved to her credit cards and banking information.

He texted Zoey, asking her if she had found

Tammy's banking information yet. Almost instantly, Zoey texted him back with an encrypted attached file. He couldn't help but smile. He really did have one hell of a team. If getting answers to this mystery was half as easy as getting answers from Zoey, they'd have Charlie in no time.

If he is alive.

Just as quickly as he thought it, he tried to strike the naysaying from his mind.

There was no sense in assuming the worst. In this case, it would only slow them down. He had to hope that Charlie was alive, and plan for the rescue. It went against his normal mantra of "hope for the best and prepare for the worst," but since the moment of learning about Charlie's existence, the worst thing he could imagine was never meeting the boy.

For that, there was no preparing.

He opened up the document that Zoey had sent, skimming through the credit-card purchases that Tammy had made for the last year. According to the statements, nine months ago she had accumulated a significant amount of debt. One month, she had owed more than 124,000 dollars on one of her cards.

What the hell?

When they had been together, she had made a point of never having any major debt. He couldn't imagine how she had gotten herself in this position. If she had needed money for Charlie, or to survive, she should've known that he would be there for her. He'd made that clear, even before he knew about Charlie.

He'd not had many relationships and Tammy knew that, and she also knew where he stood when it came to her. Why hadn't she come to him? Why hadn't she asked for help?

She didn't tell you about Charlie. If she hadn't told him about his child, then, of course, she wasn't going to tell him about any sort of financial difficulty she was having. Perhaps there were secrets about her that kept her from wanting to reach out to him. Though she had been vetted by his family before he'd started dating her, her life after him was a bit of an unknown. Clearly, she had gotten herself in trouble.

The thought broke his heart. He had only ever wanted the best for her.

"Are you okay?" Amber asked.

It was equally unsettling and amazing how Amber always seemed to pick up on his struggles. "I'll be fine, it's just challenging to see anyone you care about struggling…or having struggled." He scanned down to the next month of financial records. She hadn't used her credit card for months.

"What did Tammy do for work?" Amber asked.

"She was a corporate marketing manager. She flipped from job to job when she was younger. Last time I spoke with her she was working for Brontë Group. They are a company that work with international trade."

Amber frowned. "Did your work ever overlap with hers?"

He wasn't sure where she was going with that, but he could assume. "When we got engaged, she considered moving out here and at that time she gave up her job. She was a bit of a trust-fund kid, so she had a stable enough income that along with my income, she didn't have to work."

Looking over her financial records, it didn't appear as though she had gone back to work since they had broken up. And perhaps that was how she'd gotten into the situation she had. It surprised him that her parents hadn't taken a more active role in her finances, either. Which made him wonder if she had not told them about the baby.

If she had, her parents were old-school and probably would have pushed her to reconcile with him and pursue marriage. Perhaps that was what she had been running from. Maybe she knew that they weren't destined to be together, and she hadn't wanted to burden him with the responsibilities and requirements the child would bring to his life.

There were so many assumptions that could be made, and conjectures, but unless by some miracle he found Tammy alive, which didn't seem likely, the chance for any sort of hope for any real answers was gone.

He glanced over at Amber—she looked worn-out. "I'm so sorry about all of this. I can't imagine how you are feeling having to deal with my past and all the drama that seems to be circulating through my life. I'd like to tell you that it's normally different, and though the upheavals that I deal with don't generally come from my private life, it would be a lie to say that I am not constantly inundated by needs."

Amber reached over, taking his hand. "I can't say that I've ever had a bear case quite like this one, but I'm glad I got to help."

He appreciated that she wasn't focusing on his apology, but it couldn't be ignored even though he wanted to do nothing more than kiss her. "It's just, with everything, I don't want you getting in over your head. I know all of this goes way beyond your usual job."

She leaned across the console, her Kevlar vest rubbing hard against the computer that rested between them, making a scraping sound. She didn't seem to notice. Instead, she reached up and pressed her palm to his face and rubbed her thumb against the stubble on his cheek. "You don't need to worry about me. What you need to worry about right now is your son. Charlie needs you." She gently kissed him, stealing his breath for a moment. Having her lips against his was the only moment of peace he'd had since learning about Charlie. He wanted to hold her there, but when she pulled back, he let her go. She cleared her throat. "Now, let's go check the next GPS location."

She picked up her phone, as he struggled to find the right words. He was so grateful to have her these last few days. She was so good to him. So understanding and kind. There was a comfort in the knowledge that regardless of what happened next, they would go through it together. He could ask for nothing more.

"Hey," Amber said, frowning at him. "Did you know that there is an old, abandoned gold mine near the ranch?"

He shook his head. "How do you know that?"

She pointed back to her app. "I use the USFS mapping database, which includes geological studies. Plus, one of my friends is the lead archaeologist for the state, and he sends me points when he and his teams are working at different locations. They worked on one of the encampments associated with this mine a few years ago."

AJ smirked. "And here I thought I had cool friends. Gotta say having a friend who is an archaeologist is pretty neat."

"I don't know, running with people who travel all over the world and overthrow governments is pretty amazing. That being said, I think you'd really like my friends. Maybe someday I'll get to introduce you to them."

"I'm down for that, whenever you'd like." He loved the thought of being incorporated into her life in a more substantial way. It was funny, but he could almost imagine a life with her, walking into places and having her on his arm. He would love to show her off as his girlfriend.

Amber's smile widened. "Let's find Charlie first." She turned back to her phone. "As for the mine, I don't know how big it was, or what kind of yield it delivered. From what I have here—" she tapped on her phone "—the claim was originally filed in 1890, not long after Montana became a state. Mining at that time was really interesting. There were several methods that people used, but in this area and through this formation toward Butte, the most common method for extracting minerals from ore was through a method called leach mining."

AJ enjoyed listening to her, though he didn't really know why or how any of this information would help them. At this point, though, he was willing to delve into anything, if it led to answers.

"I've heard of leach mining. It's where they use cyanide, arsenic and other heavy metals to get gold and copper out of minerals. Right?" he asked.

"Something like that, yes." She nodded. "Companies still do leach mining now, though it is more regulated and the environmental effects, arguably, aren't as catastrophic as they were in the earlier days of mining."

She shot him a curious smile.

"What?" he asked, confused by what could have possibly made her so animated.

"I just had an idea," she said. She drew her phone to her chest as if she was trying to control herself. "You know what one of the major signs of long-term contact with arsenic is?"

He shook his head.

"Arsenic is a poison and it's been used for years as a pesticide, but when people historically working with the poison were around it for long periods of time, they would build up somewhat of a tolerance. However, they would develop rashes, odd pigmentation and dark black discoloration on their hands and feet. People can get what are called Mees' lines in their fingernails."

His thoughts jumped to Tammy's hand. Her palm had been splotchy and blackened, and her nail beds had taken on a purple-and-green hue. He couldn't recall seeing white lines on her fingernails, but he was sure it wouldn't take anything to get a picture of the remains and look.

"If there is a mine on the ranch, a leach mine with high levels of toxins, and if Tammy was there for an extended period of time—like *months*—it would explain her hand." Amber's eyes widened. "It also would explain the bear. If it had been in that cave, denning or living… Oh, my God, AJ, it all makes sense."

Chapter Seventeen

It was macabre, but Amber was thrilled at the lead they'd just got. Sure, it may well not be the answer, but it was the best theory she had come up with for the bear and the series of events that had led them to finding Tammy's remains.

She drove fast, bumping down the logging road and heading back to the ranch.

"Every point Zoey gave us has views of the ranch. Tammy was definitely scoping us out." AJ sounded a bit breathless as they hit another pothole in the road.

Amber wasn't sure if he agreed with her idea about the arsenic poisoning, but it wouldn't be hard to prove now that they had the bear's remains.

"Did your brothers get the bear to the university yet?" she asked.

He tapped on his phone. "Mike said they dropped her off about thirty minutes ago."

Amber pulled over and sent off a quick text to the lab tech she had been working with: Test stomach contents and hair for arsenic poisoning.

The woman sent her a thumbs-up in response. It was such a simple response that it almost annoyed Amber, but then she reminded herself the woman most likely had her hands full as she prepped the necropsy. She literally held the possible answers in her hands.

"One of the telltale signs of arsenic poisoning is also anorexia," AJ said, staring at his phone. "According to the CDC, it also greatly affects the neurological system."

"We need to get video from the hotel and see if there is any footage showing Tammy. Maybe we can get a better read on her physical and neurological status from the video." Amber couldn't help the wave of hope filling her that they were close to finding answers. Yet, she tried to remain calm. They still had to find Charlie.

AJ was working away feverishly on his phone; she could see he was texting Zoey and his brothers in a group chat. "Zoey is on it. I'm sure we can get the video soon, but I think she is going to have to go through Detective Baker."

"That's good, then he can let the medical examiner know to test for arsenic on Tammy's hand as well." She tapped her fingers on her steering wheel and smiled.

He was so incredible to her, and she loved his ability to talk to her and communicate as he did. It had been a long time since she had felt so at home with someone's presence. There was no denying that there was something between them, even if it was something that she couldn't act on.

He went back to his phone as she careened down the road, thinking about the samples she had taken from the bear. If need be, she could possibly do her own testing. She had always enjoyed that kind of work, but hopefully the lab would take care of everything.

As they approached the ranch, she could see there were a number of trucks missing. It appeared as though AJ's teams were on the move. It didn't take long before they were rumbling over the cattle guard near the area in which they had first gotten the hairs from the bear.

So much had happened in so little time. It was unbelievable to think that just a few days ago, AJ hadn't been a part of her life and this assignment was nothing more than an annoyance.

In all of her wildest imaginings, she would

have never thought she would have found herself here.

"Zoey let Baker know about the bear. He seemed pretty relieved, apparently. He also is sending her the video footage from the hotel. Should be here in the next hour or two." He looked down at his watch. "It's getting late, but I want to keep looking for Charlie. I don't want him to possibly be spending another night alone."

"Yeah," Amber said, thinking about the boy possibly out in the winter night by himself, but she couldn't bear the thought and she stamped it down.

"Let's swing over to the old miner's cabin and see if we can get inside. It's the only place I can think of that a toddler would have holed up on the ranch and gone unnoticed."

They drove to the belly of the ranch, where the old miner's cabin stood. In the dark, it seemed far more ominous than she remembered it, with its looping webs of horsehair moss chinking and abyssal windows.

They crunched through a layer of snow as they got out of the truck and made their way up to the cabin. AJ shone his flashlight inside as they neared the windows, but from even where she stood, she could see that the place was deserted. She opened the door but was met with only the sounds of scurrying mice. Though it was unlikely, the inside of the cabin seemed colder as the air bit at the insides of her nostrils and seemed to freeze in her lungs.

It was odd, but in finding it cold, empty and undisturbed—so far as she could tell in the dark—Amber found comfort. If the little boy had been inside, the chances he would have still been alive were dismal.

When she looked over at AJ, she could see the exhaustion on his face. The poor man probably hadn't really slept in days. Though he was tough, everything was taking a toll. "You need a break. For now, there's nothing more we can do for Charlie," she said, turning back toward the truck and leading him by the hand. "Don't worry, we will come up with something. We just need to keep digging for ideas."

He smiled, but even that looked like it had taken a strain. "I'm sure you're right."

It was a quick ride back to the ranch, but she kept glancing over at him. It hurt her to see him so road-worn, but damn if she didn't know how he was feeling. If only she could make him feel better and take some of the pain and pressure from him. She parked in front of his house. He got out and walked around to her side, opening her door for her.

"Why, thank you," she said, and he answered with an acknowledging nod.

"Of course," he said, motioning her toward his place.

He opened the door for her and held it for her as she passed by. There was something in the way they moved together that made her feel as if they were stepping into the relationship that they had both been avoiding—well, she had, more than him. Yet, she had picked this place and this moment; she was making choices that didn't align with what she was telling herself she should do, but what her heart pointed her toward.

"Do you want a drink or something?" She smiled over her shoulder at him as she walked toward his kitchen.

"I was going to say you are welcome to make yourself at home, but I can see that won't be a problem," he teased. "I'd definitely take some water." He touched her shoulder as he stepped beside her and reached up into the cupboard by the sink and grabbed a glass. He poured water into a glass and handed it to her, then did the same for himself before sitting down at the island.

He took a long drink and then ran his hands over his face, as though he could wipe away his exhaustion and disappointment in not locating Charlie.

"Why don't you go sit on the couch?" She motioned toward the overstuffed leather couch that sat in front of the fireplace a few feet from them. "I will put together a little something for us."

"You don't need to do that," he said. "You're my guest."

"Don't worry, you just go and rest. Let me take care of you for a little bit."

"I appreciate that, Amber. I got the next meal." He smiled and stood up, then, almost instinctively, he gave her a soft kiss to her cheek in thanks. He stumbled slightly as he walked toward the couch and then sat down. He turned on the television to a news channel—it seemed like it was all out of habit and she couldn't help but smile at how well they just fit together.

This could be their life. After having nearly every meal by herself in the woods or inside her truck for the last few years, it was inexplicably comforting to have this moment with a man she cared about. It was funny how the little things in life could mean more than any over-the-top expression of affection. If anything, it was the simple things and these types of moments that built a life and reaffirmed love.

She walked to the refrigerator and peeked

inside. The contents were pretty sparse, with just a pack of turkey lunch meat, bread and sliced cheese. She smiled as she took out the items and put together sandwiches for them.

Walking over, she went to hand him his plate, but his eyes were closed and she could tell from his steady, quiet breaths that he had fallen asleep.

Oh, he is so handsome, she thought, looking at his sweet face, finally relaxed in the comforting hands of sleep.

He needed this. Quietly, she put down his sandwich, walked to his room and grabbed his blanket. Bringing it out, she gently placed it over him.

It had been years since she had taken care of anyone like this, and it pulled at her in ways she didn't think possible. Something about it reminded of when she had taken care of her parents after William had died and it equally warmed and broke her heart. She hadn't talked to her parents since Thanksgiving, so she really needed to give them a call.

She made quick work of her sandwich and then turned to her phone. She started to press in a number, but then she didn't want to disturb AJ. Instead, she went to her email and started to sift through all the work issues that were piling up. Apparently, there was a herd of elk on a nearby ranch that was causing havoc on the rancher's hay. The rancher wanted permission to haze the animals away, but she always hated giving the go-ahead on that kind of thing—it opened up a can of worms when it came to the legalities and the humane treatment of animals.

After more than an hour of responding to the most pressing emails, she decided to call it a night.

She stood up and moved to AJ, then gently sat down beside him. She moved a stray piece of his hair out of the middle of his forehead as he slept. His eyelids fluttered at the sensation and he opened his eyes slightly and glanced over at her. He smiled, reached up and touched her face. He leaned over and took her lips with his.

The action was so unexpected and sweet that she melted under his touch, forgetting about the emails and the work that needed their attention. Instead, she leaned into his kiss, beckoning his tongue with her own as they nipped and played.

His kiss turned deeper and his hand moved down from her face, and he pulled her into his lap. From where she sat, she could feel him grow harder beneath her.

Without warning, he swept her up into his arms. She threw her arms around his neck as he carried her into the bedroom and gently laid her on the bed.

She pulled open his shirt and he slipped out of his pants in almost a single motion.

He moved onto the bed beside her. She reached up and started to unbutton her shirt, finding herself entranced by the heat of the moment after the drama of the day. Everything had been so stressful, so full of emotions, that this felt light—a needed moment of reprieve.

Not saying a word, he gently nudged her hands away and unbuttoned the top two buttons before pulling the shirt up and over her head.

He kissed her lips as he unclasped her bra and slipped the straps from her shoulders. The cool air hit her nipples and made her gasp in his mouth. She could feel him smile at the sound, but he didn't break their kiss.

This man... This incredible man...

His hand slipped down to her pants and he made quick work of the button and zipper before pushing them down. She wiggled and grabbed the ankles of her pants with her toes as she pulled them off, all without stopping their kiss. She never wanted to stop kissing him.

He moved down between her knees and kissed the insides of her thighs as he lay down. He lifted her legs, putting them over his shoulders as his kisses worked to her center. She quaked under the gentle pulse of his tongue, the strokes and flicks.

It... This... Him...

He traced her lips with his fingers and he gently pressed inside, humming as he penetrated her. She moaned, the sound coming from deep within her, and echoing the primal urge she felt building. His tongue was like the beat of a drum, echoing the tempo of her heart and the rasping calls of her breath.

This. Dance. Oh...

"Amber..." He moaned her name against her and it made her breath come faster.

Her body moved with him, rising and falling in cadence with his mouth.

"AJ..." she replied as she reached the point of no return and the tempo of his touch brought her to the end.

He tried to move against her, kissing away the wetness he had created, but she pushed his head away, unable to bear even the gentlest of his touches.

"Come here," she ordered, nearly breathless.

He moved to kiss her as he eased his body up hers, but she reached down and took his chin and looked him in the eyes. "I want you to kiss me," she said.

There was a sparkle in his eyes as he answered her with a devilish smile. His kiss was hard against her lips, just like the rest of him.

She licked his lips, pulling her flavor from him like she was the sweetest of lollipops.

"Amber," he said, moaning into her mouth as her body started to pulse again and hunger for more.

She reached down, wetting her hand and moving to him, and started to stroke. He was so hard. *Hard for me.*

Working his length, he grew impossibly harder in her hand and she slowed. She couldn't spend another night with him without feeling him inside. She stopped as she looked up at him. "AJ..."

His eyes were narrowed with lust and longing as he looked upon her. "Yes?" he asked, pressing against her, showing her exactly where he also wanted to go.

"Grab a condom," she said.

He moved quickly, going to his nightstand and pulling one out.

Before he had a chance to rip it open, she took it from him. "This is my job."

After ripping open the package, she took out the condom and slipped it over him, careful to not play too much so he could last inside of her. She needed to feel him. All of him. For as long as she could. She needed to remember every second of this.

He moaned as she moved him between her

thighs and eased him inside of her, lifting her hips to meet his body with hers. She gripped the sheets as he slipped out slightly and then moved deep into her, filling her to the point of sweet pain. He was so big.

This man was perfect.

He stretched and pressed into her like nothing else she had ever felt before. As he moved, he hit a spot inside of her that made her fear that she would be the one who couldn't last. She had to wait, to take him to the place he had already taken her.

She'd always thought the G-spot was a myth until now. There was something.

"Right there," she moaned, grabbing his hips and guiding his thrusts into her. "Right… There."

He made a sound, like a growl, as he took her again and again, following her body's moves and the movement of her hands.

"Amber, it's okay… I can tell—"

Before he could finish speaking, she felt her body give way.

She cried out, giving everything she was to him and for him in a way she had never given before. He followed, making the ecstasy even more exquisite as they gave themselves together. In this moment, there was only this…and only them.

Chapter Eighteen

AJ had forgotten how good it felt to wake up next to someone he cared for after a long night of lovemaking. There were few feelings in the world that could compare to the utter, blissful exhaustion that came with melding souls. That was the only way he could adequately describe what they had done.

She was his and he was hers.

There wasn't much that he could pull together for breakfast, but he had made sure to make her some fresh coffee and just about when the coffeepot was full, he made out the sound of her getting dressed from inside their room.

Their room. He smiled at the thought.

It may have been a little premature, but after what had happened between them last night, it seemed like they were both finally on the same page in really giving this relationship a chance. He loved the idea as much as he cared about Amber. While he wasn't in a hurry to take things too fast or jump into marriage, he was glad that they could finally start acting naturally on their feelings and see where they would go together.

He hummed as he poured a to-go mug for her, making sure to add a little bit of powdered creamer and some sugar. He wasn't sure exactly how she took her coffee, but just like everything else about her, he couldn't wait to learn.

Tapping on the door, he said, "I come bearing gifts."

She opened the bedroom door and gave him a kiss on the cheek as he handed her the coffee. "Thank you, honey," she said, and it was so natural that it was like they did this kind of thing every day.

He slapped her ass as she sauntered by him, ready and dressed for the day.

"So…" she said, taking a sip of her coffee and looking over the rim at him.

Damn. I am the luckiest man alive.

"So?" he asked.

"Should we talk about what happened?"

He wouldn't have been more surprised if he'd woken up in another country. He knew he shouldn't compare Amber to anyone in his past, but he'd never been with a woman who was just nonchalant about their sex life, or wanted to just casually talk about what did or didn't happen behind closed doors.

He had a feeling that maybe he was a little behind the times, or maybe it was just that he was inexperienced when it came to that kind of thing, but he liked that this would be how it was going to be between them. He liked candor and openness when it came to someone he trusted and brought into his life. That kind of honesty would be what would make their lives together.

"I'm just grateful. I have wanted to have you in my bed almost from the moment I set eyes on you. I'm honored that you would share your body with me." He leaned in and gave her a kiss on her head.

She looked up at him and took another drink of her coffee, taking in what he had said. "Babe, I knew you were an incredible man, but every second I spend with you it becomes more and more obvious that you are out of my league." She giggled.

"More like the other way around," he said, pouring himself a coffee and turning back to her. "You know, though, what may make our relationship strong is the fact that we both think we are getting someone outside our coverage area."

She snorted so hard that a little dribble of coffee dripped from her nose and she hurried to wipe it away. "What was that?" she asked between choking laughs.

"It's dumb, just a football reference. I was just trying to say that I love that we both think the other is too good for us. It means we are a perfect fit."

"Just as long as you don't expect me to be perfect, we will do fine." She smiled.

"I don't want a perfect person—it would be entirely too much pressure to keep pace with." He paused. "Plus, I've learned that the greatest times in life and in relationships come in moments when everything goes wrong. Those are the moments when you get to see a person for who they really are, not the version they want you to see."

"Yes," she said, pointing at him in agreement. "You get to see the authentic self."

"You have definitely seen me at my worst over the last few days, and for that I'm sorry. I wish you could see me at the top of my game."

She shook her head. "If this is your worst, then I think I would have been far too nervous to talk to you at the top of your game. You're the hottest man I've ever dated."

"We are dating?" He sent her a cute side-glance.

"Does that mean I can start calling you my girl-friend?"

She beckoned him over to her with the wiggle of her finger. He did as she ordered, but then she motioned to have him come even closer so she could whisper in his ear. "You are mine."

"Then girlfriend it is, or would you prefer mistress?" He gave her a playful kiss as her fingernails pressed into the skin on his chest.

Her phone buzzed on the counter next to them, pulling him from his reverie of all that was Amber. She picked it up with a sigh, like she hated that she had to give up this moment just as much as he did.

His fingertips found the place on his chest where she had marked him, almost in exactly the same spot she had just a few hours ago, when they had been in bed together. He loved the idea of being marked by her—he really was hers.

He walked into the bedroom then tidied up and made the bed while she handled whomever it was that was on the other end of the phone. After ten minutes or so, he came out, and she was thumbing the edge of her coffee mug, staring at what little was left in the cup.

"Yes. Got it. Thanks for calling," she said,

but then set the phone back down. Her face was impassive as she looked up at him.

"Everything okay?" he asked.

"That was the lab. The DNA tests came back. The bear we had in our trap was the same that had crossed your fence."

"Good, that's at least one less thing we have to worry about. We didn't need a multitude of predatory animals rolling through the ranch."

Her face tightened. "They also got the arsenic results—they came back positive. They said the animal had most likely been ingesting the toxin for a long period of time because it was also found in the hair as well as the stomach contents."

"Was that all they found, you know...in the stomach?"

She tapped the coffee cup like she was answering him in Morse code. "The animal had ingested human remains. It will be another day to see if they can get adequate DNA from the samples they took, but they believe it is likely Tammy."

He sat down on the chair next to her. He wasn't exactly surprised, but the news still wasn't easy to hear. There was no longer any doubt about this being Tammy. He had shared so much of his life with her, so many memories, and a renewed sense of grief washed over him.

For a moment, he wondered if there was anything he could have done to change the outcome, or prevent her death. If only he had called her, or reached out. Yet, there was no way that he could have known what was going to happen to her or her life. "Was there any evidence as to how she died in the contents?"

She shook her head. "It will take a bit to get that info, but I did get enough information to know that my feeling was right—there was no evidence of the bear having eaten a child. The bones ingested were that of a full-grown adult."

It felt strange to be relieved over the results of the stomach contents of a bear, but nonetheless he was, as the odds of Charlie being alive had just gotten significantly higher. Now he just had to find him.

He was filled with a renewed energy. Charlie was out there somewhere, alive. The one thing he was damn good at was locating those who were nearly impossible to track down.

"Can you please let Zoey know about the findings?" he asked, pointing toward her phone.

She nodded, then picked up her phone and sent off a series of texts and emails.

It was great having Amber around. He could get used to this. In fact, if he had his way, he would. However, Charlie first.

"AJ, come over here." She was staring intently at her phone. "I don't know if it will lead to anything, but I just did some digging and found out that there's a mine shaft near the homesteader's cabin. It connects in with a ton of other shafts, but according to the data I got, the shafts collapsed sometime in the past."

He walked over and looked at the screen with her. She'd pulled up the maps on her phone of the geological data of the area.

According to it, the mine shaft had once connected in with a trail of other shafts, one of which originated on forest service land a few miles up from the ranch. Amber pulled up the coordinates—coordinates that were strikingly close to those Zoey had given them. Either Tammy's remains had to have been brought by the bear onto the ranch, or she had to have gotten in another way...or someone had dumped her body.

Yet, if someone had disposed of her body, they wouldn't have done it on the ranch unless they wanted to set up the Spades and Martins to get in trouble for the murder.

Then again, if someone had stepped foot onto the ranch, everyone would have had to have known. Plus, it didn't explain everything. There were so many facets to this, making it as intriguing as it was infuriating.

He frowned—they needed to start by confirming the most likely connections. "So, you think those were the shafts where the bear and Tammy might have gotten into the arsenic?"

"Oh, yeah, totally. Short of a bear eating loads of bait with ant poison...it seems like the likely choice. I mean, if there is a water source down there, the bear might have been drinking from it daily. Thus, why it would be losing weight and having all the health issues it was—all added to the fact it was getting up there in age."

"That doesn't explain Tammy being there, though."

"I already thought about that. If Tammy was trying to get onto the ranch, it would be damned hard to get in and out without being noticed. Best alternative would be these tunnels."

She had a point, but he was still struggling to make sense of everything. "Why would she want to be on the ranch, though?"

His stomach dropped as he thought about what Zoey had told him about the Fellinis trying to recreate Rockwood and the bounty Frank Fellini had out on them. With everything that had happened the last few days, he hadn't been able to focus much on that threat, but maybe he should've been. "Son of a…"

"What?" Amber asked.

"We—STEALTH—have a lot of enemies. Zoey told me there are some high-powered individuals who are on the hunt to take us down."

"And you think Tammy had something to do with that?"

AJ shrugged. "It's the only thing I can think of that would make sense here—if she was working for them and trying to get information about us."

"But what does this have to do with Charlie?"

"Again, we are going to have to do some digging, but I'm going with Occam's razor here—the simplest answer is probably the right one. And there are a few things that motivate people better than anything else—love, hate and money." He put his cup in the sink, tipping out the rest of the coffee. "She loved me once, hates me now and had found herself ass-deep in debt."

"If she was in debt, I'm sure you're right. She was probably desperate to take care of Charlie. And if she hated you, it definitely makes sense why she wouldn't call and ask for help." There was a sadness in Amber's voice.

"The worst part of all of this, is that she had

to have known that I would've supported them. All I can think is that she didn't trust me with Charlie." His thoughts moved to last night, and sharing his bed with Amber. Would she figure out that he wasn't a man worth being a father or husband, as well? He wouldn't blame her if she did. They hadn't known each other long enough for her to really hate him yet, but maybe that would come.

He couldn't go through that kind of heartbreak again, and he definitely couldn't risk losing his heart. Yet, he couldn't help but feel like it was too late to make different choices. He was in too deep with Amber.

Amber put her hand on his lower back and looked up at him. "I can see you are really upset, and I don't blame you. We are going to find Charlie. When we do, you're going to have a chance of being the father you want to be."

"But what if Tammy was right?" He felt his chest tighten. "I mean, what if I'm not meant to be a father? What if I'm no good at it?"

Amber chuckled. "You do see the irony in this, don't you?"

He frowned, not following exactly what she was thinking. "What do you mean?"

"Here's a woman who was afraid of letting you be a father because of who you are and what you do, and yet she was the one who may well have been the biggest threat to your son. I'm sure she was being the best mom she could be, and doing what she had to for them to survive—and for that, she's commendable. Yet, she was putting him in situations that were probably questionable at best. I mean look, she left him somewhere to go on a hunt for you, and left you no way to find the boy."

"Maybe she didn't want me to find him. Or it could have been due to the cognitive impairment because of the arsenic. It's possible she just wasn't all there toward the end." He shrugged.

"AJ, it's also possible that we were initially right with assuming the marks on her hands were merely frostbite."

It was just so much easier to hope Tammy had been in an altered state when making her decisions. At least if that was the case, he wouldn't have to feel so bad about himself, and make assumptions about what she thought of him as a person. However, in the end, it didn't really matter what she had thought of him. What was done was done.

There was no point in revisiting the pain of the past.

He picked up his phone and texted Zoey, filling her in about their thoughts on Tammy and her motivations, and that he wanted to head down into the mine. He hated that all of this that was happening at the ranch was his doing. He was one hell of an ineffectual leader if he couldn't even keep his personal life from affecting his entire team.

Thinking about his being a father, if he did find Charlie—no, *when* he found Charlie—he would need to be the father that the boy deserved. And while his parents had been able to raise him and his siblings in this black ops world, it had definitely left a mark. Not only that, but this work had also cost his parents everything. He couldn't risk leaving the child an orphan just like his parents had left him and his siblings. Yet he knew of no other world.

Tammy was probably right—he would be a terrible father and she'd had every right to keep the boy from him. Maybe he was wrong even trying to find him. She wouldn't have left Charlie in a position where he would've been compromised, but any number of things could have changed in her life, since he'd last seen her, that would have resulted in her making this kind of decision. Clearly, things had.

His phone buzzed; Zoey had texted. He opened it up. It read: Be careful in the mine, but yeah, see what Tammy was into. Still waiting on video from Baker. Stay close.

He raised his phone for Amber to see. "We have our marching orders."

Amber nodded. Walking toward the door, he grabbed her jacket and helped her slip it on. He grabbed his keys, motioning toward his truck, then walked her to her door and helped her inside. It was strange, but before Zoey had texted, they had been so talkative with one another, but now... Nothing.

"Are you okay?" he asked. "I know this is a lot. I didn't mean to overwhelm you back there."

Amber blinked a few times like she was trying to shake off some kind of daze. "Nah, you didn't overwhelm me, but did I ever tell you *how* my brother died?"

He shook his head, but he had a sense that today was exceptionally difficult for her. She was such a courageous woman.

"I don't talk about it much, but the reason I became a game warden was because of him. William and I were best friends growing up. You know that two-kids syndrome, where the kids become besties out of necessity. We were both good students, and he was three years older than me, so when I had problems or issues, he would help me with my homework. We were each other's everything."

"Is that why you acted like you did when you

found out my team had contacted your parents?" AJ was filled with guilt. Here he had been so wrapped up in his own life and drama that he never stopped to think that everything they were doing was affecting her in a personal way.

She nodded. "My parents will never get over his death. So, I try to bring nothing negative to their life. I want to be the easy child. I never want them to worry about me."

"I'm sorry, Amber," he said. He wasn't sure whether or not he should ask what had happened to her brother, but before he had the chance, she continued.

"When he left to go to college, he went to school in Bozeman. It wasn't far from where we grew up, but it definitely provided him with some much-needed independence. And one day he was out skiing, and it was a day a lot like today, and he ended up falling in a tree well. They didn't find him until two months later. There's nothing worse than not knowing what happened to a loved one. So, I understand how you're feeling."

"Why didn't you tell me this before?" he asked.

"You already had enough going on. It happened ten years ago. There's no going back and changing it. And when you're going through something like this, the last thing you need, especially when you're in the thick of it, is someone telling you about a death in their family. He was actually the one that was going to school to be a wildlife biologist. I followed in his footsteps, in his memory."

He wanted to be mad at her, for keeping this a secret from him. However, he could understand her line of thinking. "That's amazing that you did that for him and your family." He paused, thinking about his own crew. "You know, one of my biggest fears is to lose someone I love."

Her eyes welled with tears, but she rapidly blinked them away. "I can understand why you'd never want to experience anything like it. It has a way of ripping a family apart—it changes everything."

"That I can believe. The Martins lost a sister. They still talk about her—she died in the line of duty. I know they still struggle." He reached over, took her hand and gave it a kiss. "I know things will be hard sometimes. Yet, if we're going to be together, remember—no secrets. Okay?"

She gave him a simple smile. "I'll try. Just know that today, going into the places that may or may not have been where your ex died, it brings up a lot of weird stuff for me. I thought I'd be fine. And... I will be. Just be patient."

"I promise to always try and be patient. No matter what is going on."

He held her hand as Amber pointed him in

the right direction of the mine-shaft entrance near the homesteader cabin. Before this week, he hadn't spent a great deal of time out in the woods on the property, but now that he was, he had to admit it was a beautiful place.

"According to my map," Amber said, pointing at her phone, "the mine shaft was located about fifty yards from the cabin." She stepped out of his pickup and started walking to the west of the cabin.

He followed behind her, just trying to catch up. She kicked away the snow on the ground as she moved around the area.

Not far from where he stood, there was an odd shape in the snow. It was probably nothing but he moved closer to check it out. Scratching away the snow, he discovered a large hole. It had to be the entrance to the mine shaft. "Amber," he called, "I found it."

He cleared away more of the snow, and she looked at him with an excited smile. "You did it." She threw her arms around his neck, like they had just found the answer to all their questions. And yet, as she held him, and he held her, he couldn't help but feel that their search had only just begun.

Chapter Nineteen

There was the sound of dripping water coming from deep inside the belly of the earth as they made their way down into the tunnels. Amber was behind him, but AJ doubted that she would let him take the lead for long.

The light on his phone reflected off the icy walls and mirrored down the shaft, making it less ominous than he would have expected. The shaft was about eight feet wide in most places, as though it had been constructed for a donkey loaded down with ore to pull a cart in and out of the mine. If he sat still long enough, he wondered if he could hear the echoes of the bygone era and the animals that made it all possible.

If they hadn't been down there looking for evidence of Charlie, he might have almost thought being in the mine was pretty damn cool. As kids, he and his brothers would have gone gangbusters in a place like this, playing army and shoot-'em-up games while giving their parents a reprieve from their constant mischief.

The thought made him smile. It also reminded him of Amber's brother and the loss that must have been so hard on her and her family. No wonder she hadn't wanted to talk about it, but now she definitely made a lot more sense to him. She wasn't independent because she wanted to be, she was that way out of necessity.

He'd seen what happened to families after a loss of a child. It was difficult for everyone, and parents found themselves guilt-ridden and lost. Parenting of other children either became the primary focus to the point of being overbearing and repressive, or, in their sadness, they lost sight of the remaining child or children.

Either way, Amber had been dealt a tough hand.

If he had his way, she would never find herself hurt like that again. He would do anything to keep her safe and protected.

She stepped beside him like she could tell that he was thinking about her and she slipped her hand into his.

He loved that she would just take what she needed from him, but he should have known that she would have liked to hold his hand. Giving her fingers a little squeeze, he asked, "Are you doing okay?"

She nodded. "Caves are definitely not my kind of thing. I prefer knowing there is sky over my head." She moved closer to him as they continued to walk. "Did you know that Montana has more than seven hundred earthquakes a year?" She glanced up at the earthen ceiling above them.

"It's going to be okay," he said, but as he did, he couldn't help but be reminded that these tunnels had caved in and not that long ago he had heard about a sinkhole in a school playground when a mine shaft gave way.

He tried to start walking faster, but gently, so to not draw any unnecessary alarm.

It would all be okay. The ground was frozen.

Then there was the sound of another drip.

He wasn't sure how the ground above them could be frozen and there was still water dripping, but it did nothing to comfort him.

After walking for another ten minutes or so, he was tempted to turn around. This place was admittedly dangerous, and they were already aware it was full of toxic chemicals. Add on the danger of being caved in on… Yeah, they needed to get out of here.

"AJ," Amber said, stopping. "Look."

There, on the ground at their feet, was a large tuft of griz hair. It was matted together with dried blood and as he crouched down to get a better look, he saw the hair had the roots still intact.

The floor of the cave was covered in dirt and gravel, and ahead of them a few feet was a rock, about the size of a man's fist, covered in blood and more bear hair.

"Do you think…?" He paused, looking up at Amber as the reality of the scene started to soak into his senses.

He stood up and took a long series of breaths.

Amber put her hand on his back. "AJ, it's okay. You're okay."

Nodding, he couldn't pull his gaze off the rock that was covered in blood. At least Tammy had fought back. She probably used the cobble to hit at the bear while it was attacking. His thoughts twisted to what her last moments must have been like, the bear coming at her, starved and half-mad in the underbelly of the earth. He couldn't imagine much more hellish of a scenario. There was no way she could have made it out of this alive. Their suspicions had been right—she was dead.

He caught himself wishing that she'd had a swift end, but looking at the rock, he knew that wasn't likely the case.

"Oh, baby," Amber said, reaching up and wiping away a tear that had slipped from him without him even being aware.

"Sorry, I swear I'm not the kind of guy who loses his crap like this…" He rubbed the base of his palm against his forehead as if he could strike the emotions from him. Yet, no amount of rubbing would erase the scene before them.

"AJ, it's okay. I know your relationship wasn't perfect with her, but you loved her. Seeing this has to be so hard for you." She leaned against him. "I'm just glad that I'm here to help you through this, but if I could, I would take this pain away and do this for you."

"But you hate caves," he said, trying to joke.

"Not going to lie, I hate them even more now, but that doesn't change the fact that there isn't a thing that I wouldn't do for you. You deserve to be loved and cared for, and I don't know if you are aware, but your pain is my pain. Seeing you hurt like this, hurts me."

Her words both warmed him and yanked at his heart. He stepped to face her and pulled her into his arms. "I hope you know I feel exactly the same way about you. We will get through this. It's hard and it hurts, but at least this way we know exactly what caused Tammy's death. I don't have to wonder anymore."

Amber hugged him tight, pressing her face against his chest.

Nothing with Amber was ever going to be very easy…except having feelings toward her. That was the easiest thing that had ever come to him in his life.

She stepped out of his arms and put her hand back in his. "Let's keep looking—maybe we can find the rest of Tammy's remains."

His stomach sank as he was pulled back to the reality of their situation. Yes, they needed to get out of this hell.

She moved the light of her phone back and forth as they pressed deeper into the cave. They walked slowly, passing by several bear tracks where the animal must have scratched at the dirt, or possibly where it had been running.

He couldn't imagine what Tammy had been doing down here. It was dark and foreboding, and apparently home to a top apex predator. It was hard telling what else could have been found here, and she had never been the kind he would have expected to just adventure into a place like this.

Hiking around a bend in the cave, they came to a large cavern. Flashing his light in the direction of the walls, he spotted a number of man-size metal cases. Amber shot him a look and they walked over toward them.

The one nearest him was latched closed. There wasn't any dust accumulated on the top. On the side of the boxes were a series of barcodes and labels. He leaned in and read what appeared to be a shipping label—addressed to Tammy Reynolds at the Red Lion hotel.

For a second, his mind went to a dark place. At times in the past, he'd heard of troops running into traps like these, and when they moved the box or opened them, they had been blown up. Had Tammy set up a bomb for him or his family?

No.

These are just boxes.

Under the ranch.

Where she was trespassing and possibly spying.

He tried to think of something else that was inside the boxes, but his mind kept circling around the idea of this being a bomb.

He glanced around the cavern. On the other side of the cave were more boxes. They were of varying sizes, but most were so large that he wondered how she had gotten them down here. There was no way she could have carried them in. He hadn't seen a cart or any tire tracks, but looking around the room, there were several tunnels that ran into this room. It was possible this was the main hub within the mine.

Amber let go of his hand and walked across the cave, her footfalls making a crunching sound on the gravel and dirt. He turned back, thinking about the boxes. Taking a few steps, he noticed a brown purse sitting on the ground behind one of the smaller boxes.

He picked it up and sat it gingerly on top of the blue, metal box next to him. He zipped it open—inside was a wallet and cell phone.

He pulled out the wallet. Tucked inside of it was Tammy's driver's license and a number of different debit and credit cards.

The cell phone was off, but he pressed the button and it lit up, but as it started it died.

Jackpot.

Chapter Twenty

It took far less time to hike out of the mine than it had going in. Aside from the cell phone, AJ was careful to leave everything in its place for Baker, and had chosen not to open the metal boxes. It was one hell of a comfort to know that with what they had just found everyone would be cleared of any possible wrongdoing.

Well, except for Tammy, but her mistakes had cost her desperately.

Getting in the pickup, he took out his charger and plugged in Tammy's phone.

Amber stood outside the truck. Her cell had been buzzing from the moment they had stepped into the light. From the tight look on her features as she pressed her phone to her ear, she wasn't pleased.

She motioned at him that she would be a minute, then turned her back and walked out toward the timberline.

He texted Zoey about the phone. As usual,

she was quick to answer and told him to bring it up to the office. AJ tried to give Amber her privacy, but as she paced, he wondered what was upsetting her.

Ten minutes later, Amber walked back and got into the pickup. There was a tired look in her eyes.

"Everything okay?" he asked.

"I don't want to talk about it." She stared out the window of the pickup. "I need to get back, though."

He nodded, putting the truck in gear and heading back toward the main house. He couldn't imagine what had just transpired, but his gut was telling him it had something to do with him.

He opened his mouth to speak several times, but each time her body tensed and he shut up.

Everything had been going so well between them, and now she was basically giving him the silent treatment. It didn't make sense, but maybe she was just working through something and trying to figure out a way to tell him about it.

He wasn't sure how to get her to talk, but when he was in one of those moods, or had a firestorm at work, sometimes he just had to work things through in his mind before he could talk to others.

Regardless, it was a long drive back.

Zoey stood outside the office when they pulled up to the house and she had a huge smile on her face as she waved.

He picked up Tammy's cell. The thing was girlie, complete with a flower-encrusted case with a rose gold phone inside. It said it was half-charged, but it would at least be enough to get it to turn on. Unplugging it, he got out of the pickup.

Before he could close the door, Amber turned toward him. "I need to run back to my cabin and grab my things."

"What's going on?" He leaned against the truck door.

Amber gave a tired sigh. "You don't need to worry about my stuff. Just go and take care of the phone."

He was burning to get the phone to Zoey, but he also didn't want to fail Amber.

"Go," she said, but there was a touch of annoyance in her tone.

"Okay," he said, not wanting to upset her further. "Are you leaving the ranch or coming back when you're done at the cabin?"

She chuffed. "I don't know yet, AJ. All I know is that if I don't do what I need to do, my job is going to be on the line."

"If you need me, I'll be right here." AJ

pointed toward the house. "Go ahead and take my pickup down to the cabin if you want." He tossed her the keys.

She grabbed them. "Yeah, thanks. I'll leave it parked down there."

He stared at her, wanting to ask but not wanting to pry as she scooted over into the driver's seat. He closed the driver's door and gave her a quick wave. She drove off, not looking back.

He made his way to Zoey, and she was frowning. "What is going on there?"

He looked in the direction of the truck, afraid that if Zoey watched him, she would see how confused he was. "She said she needed to run down to the cabin."

Luckily, as he turned back to Zoey, she just shrugged and didn't seem concerned about what was or wasn't going on between him and Amber. "Do you have the phone?" she asked, extending her hand and motioning for him to hand it over.

He gave it to her. "It's half-charged, but the screen was working."

"Great. That will make this all a hell of a lot easier." She turned on the phone as they walked inside.

Going to her computer, she hooked it up and set to work on her keyboard.

"Did you call Baker?" he asked, watching as she typed away as she worked to unlock the phone.

She nodded. "He was definitely curious about what was in the boxes down there. And he said to make sure to tell you he was glad you didn't disturb the scene."

He dipped his head in acknowledgment. "I'm just glad we got some answers."

Zoey tapped on the phone. "Hopefully this will help us find out why she was on the property and maybe it can even lead us in the direction of Charlie."

Hope wasn't even the tip of the iceberg of how badly he wanted and needed those answers. "So, your tech teams haven't had any sightings of him?"

"Lots of possibilities and I've been working through them. The problem is that at two years old, there is a lot of the same-shaped faces. We get a lot of false hits. Slow work."

"What about Tammy's credit cards and all that?"

"Again, we are working on it, but so far we've not had any luck." Zoey looked over at him and pushed her blue hair out of her eyes. "You know there isn't a damned thing I will stop at when it comes to protecting kids."

He was filled with the strange sensation of

gratitude, but also disappointment at the lack of progress.

Patience.

"Why don't you jump on that computer, there?" she said, pointing at a laptop on the corner of her desk. "It should be on the page you need."

He sat down in an extra rolling chair and pressed a key, and the screen turned on. He was met with the image of a chubby-faced, blond boy who was sucking his thumb as he looked up from his stroller. The photo was slightly grainy, like it had been taken from a distance. If this was the quality of the images they were working with as they looked for Charlie, what she had said made sense. This was an uphill battle.

As he tried to decide whether or not the boy was Charlie, he couldn't help but admit that he didn't really know the face he was looking for. Aside from the picture that Zoey had printed off for him, he had never actually seen his son. Though he had nearly memorized the almond-shaped blue eyes and his toothy smile, he wasn't completely sure he would be able to identify him.

The realization broke his heart.

He flipped through a series of pictures of children, picking each apart. Some were definitely not Charlie, but there were a few that he pinned to look at again. According to the information provided, one he wasn't sure of was located in Abilene, Texas, and the other was in Southampton, England.

It killed him that his child could have been anywhere in the world.

Zoey cleared her throat. "AJ, you need to come look at this."

He rolled over to her. She held up the home screen of Tammy's phone. She clicked on messages and pulled up a text from an unnamed number.

The text read: Ms. Reynolds, I need an update.

It was followed with another: Update, Ms. Reynolds.

Chills slipped down his spine as Zoey looked up at him.

"I ran the phone number," she said. "Of course, it came back as unknown, but I dug. It was going through a spoofing app—an app not frequently used, but downloaded to a phone located in Montana."

"Whose phone?" he asked.

Zoey shook her head. "I haven't gotten that far yet. Running it through the system now, may take a little bit. All I managed to pull was a digital signature on the device. I'm going to have to pull some strings to get the owner's info."

"Do you have any clue if this contract they are talking about is that bounty on STEALTH?" he asked.

"If I had to bet, I'd say it is." Zoey tapped on the keyboard. "Tammy had deleted all the other texts in the conversation, but I think I can probably get them back with a little more time and some elbow grease."

As she spoke, a text popped up on Tammy's phone: Charlie depends on you.

"I'm going to kill them," AJ said, not even waiting to think about what it would take or who it was that had his boy. It didn't matter. He would find them, and when he did, he would have blood on his hands.

Chapter Twenty-One

Amber's phone rang again just as she was stuffing the last bits of her clothing into her go bag and zipping it up. She'd had enough of her lieutenant, and that was without this third phone call. Apparently, using governmental maps to find and access the privately held mines had been a breach of protocol—a policy she hadn't known and wasn't aware of, but had gotten her in trouble nonetheless.

She should have known that the mineral rights and the mining claim were not a part of the Widow Maker Ranch and the STEALTH complex, but it hadn't occurred to her—in their search for answers—that this kind of thing would have caused a problem. Rather, she had seen a need and fulfilled the need. Now it was her neck that would be taking the axe.

If only she hadn't clocked in to the computer for the day, they would have not had grounds for dismissal. She wasn't sure exactly how, or if they were going to fire her for trespassing on private property without consent for search or a search warrant, but this was far outside her normal working parameters. Still, she had definitely screwed up.

Her bosses had every right to be upset with her, but since she had been a game warden, it was the first major screwup on her record. In fact, normally she went above and beyond the call of duty.

And here she had been thinking that she would be getting an "atta girl" for her work on the bear and discovering the truth of the attack and Tammy's resulting death.

She picked up the phone, telling herself to stay strong as she answered. "Hello, Lieutenant King. I'm just heading out now. I'll be at your office within an hour or so."

"It's fine, Sergeant Daniels. You don't need to come down to the regional offices. We have decided to put you on administrative leave, pending a thorough investigation by the regulatory board. As you know, Daniels, this is going to be a tough one to make it out of. If I were you, I'd be brushing up on my résumé. In the meantime, you need to return all state-issued gear within the next day or two."

She swallowed back the lump that had

started to form in her throat. "Sir, I'm sorry for any perceived mistakes or breaching protocol. It was not my intention."

"Stop right there, Daniels. Ignorance is not a defense."

"What does it hurt that we were inside the mine?" she countered, not waiting for him to continue his tirade.

There was a pause on the other end of the line. "The mine owners have ties that run deep. They made a call and the higher-ups had to do what they felt was required. Rest assured that thanks to you, others' heads are going to roll. If anything criminal comes from what you found, you may have very well just caused us a lot of headaches."

Of course, that's what they're worried about—legal headaches...

Her stomach ached with guilt and embarrassment. Not only was this misstep going to cost her the job that meant so much to her, but she was also going to have to tell the STEALTH team what had transpired. Her guilt and mistakes were going to be public knowledge on a grand scale.

That was all to say nothing about the effect it would play on her private life. AJ would be supportive, but it would affect everything between them. In fact, if it wasn't for him and the blinding effects her feelings for him had on her, she wouldn't have found herself in this position.

Though logically she was aware that she shouldn't, and couldn't, really be upset with him for her stepping into the wrong, she found she was still angry with him. He had to have known that his family didn't retain the mineral rights to the area, and therefore they couldn't legally access the mine shafts beneath. If he didn't, there had been enough time for him to check in with Zoey to see if there would be any conflict.

"Amber?" her boss asked, sounding as though he had been waiting for an answer to a question she hadn't heard.

"What was that?" she asked, anger lashing within her like a loose live wire.

"I will be awaiting the return of your things to the headquarters no later than five tomorrow evening. Does that work for you?"

No. It didn't work for her. None of this worked for her, but she didn't have a real choice.

"Fine." She cleared her throat. "Please set aside some time for me tomorrow morning. I'm going to need to speak to you in private regarding all of this."

There was a pause; he probably wanted to

tell her there was no use. That he wasn't the one pulling the strings on this, but he remained quiet. Finally, he said, "I really do appreciate all that you do, Amber. If it was up to me, we would be sweeping this under the rug. Your heart was in the right place and good things came from your work. Unfortunately, this is coming from the top down."

As hard as she had worked in this job and regardless of all the advancements she had made and animals and people she had helped, it disgusted her that when push came to shove, all that mattered was politics. Right there was the problem with every governmental job. There was no real loyalty—there couldn't be, because everyone was just a cog in a machine that would limp along with or without a person.

"Yep, got it. I'll see you tomorrow," she said, hanging up her phone. Though she knew she was mishandling this, she couldn't help the rage and bitterness that filled her.

She would be the first to admit she had screwed up, but in doing what she had done, she had only helped...and stepped on toes. Even though everyone close to this understood and would have probably done the same damn thing, in the end, it wouldn't really matter. She was fired.

She grabbed her go bag, then went outside and threw it in the back seat of the pickup. She was going to have to run back to her place and take out everything that belonged to her before she left for headquarters tomorrow. On top of that, she wasn't even sure how she would get home after she returned the rig. She could ask AJ, but at the thought the live wire within her sparked.

No, he had gotten her into this mess.

That left her with asking her mother.

Great.

She would have to tell them what happened, if that was the case. There was no way she would want to go into detail about her life. They would make a huge deal about what had happened and want to know everything—and she wasn't sure that she wanted to tell them about AJ.

If she did, first, she would have to get over being pissed at him for this, but on top of that it would also imply a depth in their relationship that she had started to feel, but she wasn't sure he reciprocated.

She should have never been so quick to trust him. Getting close to AJ had been against her better judgment, but she had allowed her heart to lead. She was definitely a fool when it came to men, and this was one man who was damn good at making her feel like the most special woman in the world.

She stepped on the gas pedal, a little too hard for what the conditions allowed, and the back end of the pickup fishtailed as she roared out of her parking spot and got onto the main ranch road.

She was tempted to keep going and roar out of this ranch and never look back, as she thought about the mine. There were too many questions for her to just ignore them, and she parked in front of the main office. She had to talk to Zoey.

She got out of the truck, and tapped on the door of the office. She was met with the sound of AJ's voice. "Yeah, we're here."

His voice made her stomach clench and she was tempted to turn around, but she wasn't one to run when things got tough.

She opened the door and made her way inside. Zoey was sitting behind her computer, typing away. She barely looked up as Amber came inside.

AJ's face erupted into a wide, genuine smile, but as quickly as it showed up, it disappeared and was replaced by a deep look of pain. It hit her that they had no idea what had just happened in her life, and as angry and hurt as she was, she wanted to lash out and tell them everything.

She glanced at the laptop that was open next

to her. On the screen was the picture of a little boy who looked similar to the picture she had seen of Charlie. She could tell that she had missed something in their search for the boy.

"What happened to him?" she asked, staring at the pained expression on AJ's face.

As mad and confused by everything as she was, she couldn't stop herself from worrying about him.

"Charlie is with the people who put out the bounty on us," AJ said, his voice cracking. "They are going to kill him. They think Tammy reneged on her deal with them."

The blood rushed from her face and her body turned cold. They couldn't hurt the baby. Charlie was innocent. They had to get him to safety, now. "What was the deal?"

"That, we don't quite know." Zoey turned to face her. "I'm working on trying to dig up all of Tammy's deleted messages to find out, but it's possible I won't be able to find them. The person she was talking to was using an app called TextZap. It is a spoofing app. Once things are gone, I'm thinking they are gone, unless I can hack into the provider's network and pull up the last thirty days of information. Even then, we may not get what we need."

"Have you tried texting the people back?"

Zoey grumbled, sounding annoyed. "I considered it, but only as a last resort."

"Just do it." Amber smiled as she felt some of her anger toward them dissipate. "Here, hand me the phone."

Zoey disconnected the device from her computer and handed it over. "What are you going to say?"

"I'm going to ask them when and where they want to meet for the handoff."

"Handoff of what?" AJ asked.

Amber shrugged. "I have no idea, but they clearly are waiting on something and they still think Tammy is alive. For the moment, we need to take advantage of their ignorance. At the very least, we have a chance to know where Charlie will be and when we can find him."

"A lot of things can go wrong with that plan," Zoey countered.

"Yeah," Amber conceded, "but it's better than inaction."

AJ nodded. "Damn, do I know that. It's gonna be a hell of a lot easier to pivot while moving than while rooted."

Amber smiled over at him, thankful that he seemed on her side with this, though she hadn't really expected him to be any other way—not when it came to Charlie. If they didn't get their hands on Charlie, all they had been working for, all they had done and all the sacrifices they had made would be in vain.

If they got Charlie, at least she would have lost her job for a reason.

She tapped on the phone's screen, sending off the text.

Her heart was pounding as she looked up at AJ and Zoey. "Now we wait."

Zoey sighed, but Amber couldn't decide if it was out of anger or just her being resigned to the fact that their moves were limited.

She put down the phone on the desk next to her.

Zoey took the phone and tapped on the screen, reading the text. She seemed satisfied by the simple words: I'm ready. Where and when?

They didn't have to wait long. The phone buzzed with a reply: One hour.

A second text hit the phone—a GPS coordinate.

Though things were still in the air, and there was a chance everything could go wrong, they were a step closer to saving a life and Amber couldn't help but feel a little excitement. However, it was met with resistance as she thought about what had just happened back at the cabin.

"Zoey," she asked, not sure how she would

breach the subject with them without actually letting what happened to her career slip.

"Yeah?" Zoey was punching in the GPS coordinates as they spoke.

"Does your family own the mineral rights to the ranch?" Amber asked, trying not to give it any sort of inflection that would raise an eyebrow.

It didn't work.

As she glanced over at AJ, he was studying her. "Why would you ask that?"

She shrugged, thinking about the moment when he had made her promise that she wouldn't keep any secrets from him. "I was just wondering."

He looked perturbed, like he knew she was trying to avoid any kind of real answer, and she was forced to look away.

"Zoey?" she asked, hoping to relieve some of the pressure.

"I think we do, but I'd have to look."

She nibbled at her bottom lip as she considered what to say. "I think you guys may have a problem. From what I've managed to learn in the last little bit, there is another company that owns the mining and mineral rights to the mine that sits partially under this ranch."

"What?" Zoey stopped typing and looked up at her. "That's not possible."

"If you look up mining claims, we could figure

it out in a matter of minutes. The mine was once called the J-Bar-P claim." She walked over to Zoey's computer as she turned to face the screen.

Zoey tapped away, pulling up mining claims and plat maps within a matter of minutes.

AJ stepped beside her, putting his hand on her shoulder. She loved the feeling of his touch, even if there were so many mixed emotions that came with being so close to him.

"Are you freaking kidding me?" Zoey said, slapping the desk hard with her hand. "How did you find out?" She glared over at her. "How did they get away with this?" She jabbed a finger at the screen.

"Who owns it?" AJ asked, leaning in toward the screen trying to make sense of what Zoey was raging over.

"J-Bar-P is in a holding company, but there are direct ties—albeit, not legally binding ones—to the Fellini family." Zoey spat out the name. "I knew they probably knew where we were located by now, but this is complete and utter nonsense."

Zoey closed her eyes and ran her hands over her face. "We need to get off this ranch. If that mine belongs to the Fellinis, then we are in incredible danger."

Chapter Twenty-Two

AJ's stomach hurt. He had been conditioned to withstand incredible amounts of pressure and still be suited to lead, but that was before the ranch was in danger and his son's life was on the line.

Everything had just become so real…and they had just had the rug pulled out from under their feet.

Their location had been exposed and there was a bounty on their heads. There was no way they could come back to this ranch in Montana. The bastards had taken his home, his freedom and his child.

They would pay…and he would give his last breath to get his boy to safety.

It had been hard grabbing all of his things and hitting the road as soon as they had learned that Fellini had gained access to them. Zoey had taken a sledge to the computer's hard drives, making sure to leave nothing behind when their enemies descended…and they would most certainly descend.

Baker was standing beside Amber and they were talking as he glanced over at the detective's Suburban. Baker had been unusually stoic when they had told him about everything. Yet, the detective had made sure to make it clear that they were welcome to pool resources and improvise as required, in order to get Charlie.

Troy and Mike were standing with a few of their contractors. They were wearing snow-based camo and waiting for orders from him, but before he could take action, he had to take care of a few last-minute things. They were definitely down to crunch time and if they didn't move into their positions quickly, their trap would fail.

Baker's phone rang and the man answered. Amber excused herself and made her way over to him and Zoey. "What did Baker have to say?"

Amber pinched her lips. "He has unmarked police cars in both directions coming and going from this road. A mile out from the meeting point, they have guys with Stop Sticks ready to deploy, if necessary."

"Good," AJ said, turning to Mike and giving him a nod.

Mike tipped his head and turned back to his men. They were going to take the high points, readying their rifles from a variety of points in the event a firefight broke out.

"Baker also recommended that I put on some clothes he brought. They found some of Tammy's things in the hotel room, and he thinks I can pull off her look. It might give us a few more minutes to exchange Charlie."

Goddamn, AJ loved when things started to come together in a way that was advantageous to his team and their goals.

"Great." AJ smiled.

Zoey was working on her phone. She hadn't smiled since the moment their cover had been blown, but he could understand why.

"Did you find anything?" he asked.

Zoey shook her head. "No, but I have arranged for travel for us as soon as we can hit the runway." She glanced at Amber and then to AJ, silently questioning whether or not Amber should be coming along.

He didn't know what to say or how to react, so instead he pretended not to have seen the silent gesture. Amber wasn't looking at them; instead, she was turned toward Baker, who was stepping out of his truck.

He wanted to bring Amber to wherever they were going to end up once this handoff with Charlie was over and they had to be on the move to escape the Fellini threat, but it seemed wrong to ask her to run away with him. Besides, she had her own job and her own life to take into consideration.

No matter what had happened between them, she would never want to give up everything for him—including her brother's legacy and a world she had built for her family. And he couldn't ask that of her. He cared about her too much.

Baker sauntered toward them carrying a gym bag. "Here you go." He handed Amber the bag. Taking it, she headed toward the bushes to change and Baker turned to him. "So, my bomb team just called. They have been working down in that mine. Those boxes you found…looks like they are full of C-4 explosives. Whoever they belong to better be ready for federal prison."

"Holy crap," Zoey said, finally looking up from her phone.

"You can say that again," Baker said, nodding. "You guys are damned lucky Amber uncovered this place. Though, it sounds like her job is a goner."

"What?" AJ coughed out. "What are you talking about?" He looked in the direction in which Amber had disappeared.

"Yeah, the higher-ups are pretty upset with her. Apparently, she didn't get the appropriate warrants. Your girl is going to be out." Baker paused. "I asked her for her help on this case and she did uncover one hell of a massive bomb and saved a helluva lot of lives. In an attempt to help, I made some calls to help her out, but minds are made up."

Why hadn't she told him that she'd been fired? Had that been why she had been acting off ever since she had run down to her cabin?

She didn't have to be embarrassed about losing her job, or anything else.

"She deserves a damned award, not to get canned," AJ growled. "We were sitting ducks down there and we didn't have a clue. We owe her our lives."

"I can't argue any different. I think it's a load of bull-pucky, too." Baker sighed.

Zoey didn't look back up from her phone and her fingers were nearly a blur as she typed. "Don't worry, I'm on it now. Let's just say that her bosses are going to get the ass-chewing of a lifetime from ranks and people they didn't even know existed. They won't walk right for weeks."

AJ was equally relieved and oddly sad. For a half second, he and Amber had the chance to make things work. It was selfish of him to even imagine, but if she didn't have a job, she could join their team and hit the road with them. She was so goal-oriented and dedicated to her work that she would be a tremendous asset when it came to operating the company.

Baker's phone buzzed. He tapped on the screen. "Looks like my spotters just located Fellini. He is driving a white Silverado north. They are thinking he will be at the meeting point in ten minutes. You guys need to get into position."

Amber came walking out of the bushes. He did a double take at her wearing Tammy's tight blue jeans and a button-up white collared shirt with turquoise buttons and a heavy wool jacket. She had a cowboy hat on and her hair was down. She looked entirely too much like the Tammy he had known, the one who could dress up for a honky-tonk on Saturday night and wear the same clothes to work on Monday.

Though, if truth be told, Amber did a hell of a lot better filling out every curve of those jeans. His mouth watered just looking at her.

She was pulling at the collar of the shirt as she made her way over to them. "Well, everything fit, but this coat is tight as hell." She looked over at him and gave a little laugh.

"Tight can be a good thing. It looks good on you," he teased.

Zoey turned and started walking back toward her ranch pickup.

"Are you okay with staying back?" Amber lifted the bottom of the white shirt so he could see that she was carrying a gun. "I won't be going in there unarmed."

"I'm not worried about how you will carry yourself if this all hits the fan. I'm just hoping that we can get you and Charlie out of there without an incident."

Amber pursed her lips as she looked at him. "We both know things aren't going to go well here. I don't have anything that they are hoping to get—I don't know what update they were after."

"I'm sure it had to do with the massive bomb that they had Tammy plant under the ranch."

Amber's eyes widened. "The what?"

"Oh, you heard me. Those boxes we found were full of explosives." He let out a stressed little chuckle. "I'm glad I didn't go ahead and open them while we were down there. Who knew finding a woman's purse would be the one thing that probably saved our lives? Well… that, and you. Baker told us you got fired."

"Not fired," she said, her cheeks turning red as she wiggled her finger. "I was put on administrative leave. Totally different."

He smiled. "Well, regardless… I know what you did for me…for *my family*," he said, barely managing to get the words out. The realization of all she'd done for him—what she was still doing—threatened to overwhelm him.

She squeezed his hand gently. "I know how much they mean to you. And now, I expect to do everything I can to bring your son safely into your arms as well." He knew she meant it, and it made her that much more special to him. "If I lose my job because of what I've chosen to do, then so be it. At least I left on my own terms and all while being a good person." She was a good person…and he loved her for it. The truth of that hit him as she continued, "If the government or the lawmakers don't like it, well… I will deal with that when the time comes—"

Without thinking, he pulled her into his arms and kissed her lips, knocking off her hat.

He didn't care.

Their lips melded hard and hungry against each other, no more reservations or withholding. He was hers. "Amber," he said, pressing his forehead against hers, "I love you. I can't tell you enough."

"I love you, too. No matter what happens out here today, know that I am doing this on my own accord. I want to do the right thing. I couldn't save my brother, I couldn't fix my family, but I can stop yours from being destroyed." She kissed his lips gently. "And when this is all over, I want to stay with you."

He put his hands on her face and looked deeply into her eyes. They were full of love, love he was sure was mirrored by his own. "You absolutely will, Amber. You will be my wife."

Chapter Twenty-Three

Five minutes later, Amber was standing at the meeting point. She'd driven Tammy's Pathfinder to the handoff, watching the little spinning picture of sunsets that hung from the rearview mirror nearly the whole time. Tammy had loved her son, there was no denying that, but she couldn't understand how the woman had gotten herself into such a bad position.

She pulled down the cowboy hat low on her forehead, slipping on a pair of sunglasses for just a little extra disguise. Amber doubted that Luca Fellini would be foolish enough not to recognize the fraud she was, but her safety wasn't what was paramount.

Besides, if things went wrong, she had the comfort of knowing that at any one time, there were at least four guns pointed directly at their enemy's center mass. One false move and the bastard would be going down.

He definitely deserved it. Anyone who

wanted to hurt a child deserved the most painful of deaths.

A white Silverado pulled up across the parking area off the little trailhead in the middle of the woods. The truck's engine echoed in the stillness of the snowy trees and mountains around her.

Her heart thrashed in her chest and the world seemed to slow to the point that out of the corner of her eye she watched a single snowflake spin and drift down to the ground. It was a strange thing that happened to the human mind when facing incredible stress.

She was one decision and one misstep from death, yet she wasn't afraid, was only at attention.

A dark-haired man stepped out of the pickup, a man she recognized from the pictures AJ had shown her as Luca Fellini. He was wearing a large coat that was still crisp and bright black, like it had just come off the rack of one of the sporting-goods stores in the city.

"Ms. Reynolds?" the man asked, his words rolling from him with an Italian accent.

"Where's Charlie?" she asked, trying to keep from speaking any more than necessary.

Luca smiled, his actions so far off from what she expected that she wanted to smack the look off his face. Then she remembered who she was supposed to be and whom Tammy had been working for.

"He did very well. Loves his pasta and gravy." Luca walked to the door behind the driver's seat and opened it. "Don't worry about his dirty face, he's been eating on the way to see his mama." The way he said the word tore at her heart.

This boy's mother had died. In a moment, the boy would know that she was a fraud. There would be no faking it for much longer.

There were the sounds of Luca unclipping Charlie's car seat. The little boy was talking and giggling in a language she recognized was English, but she couldn't make out the words. Her heart pounded in her chest.

He lifted the boy out, holding him so that Charlie faced away as he walked toward her. The little one turned and peeked a glance back at her before burying his face in Luca's neck. It made her wonder how long it had been since Charlie had been with his mother, that instead of holding out his arms to her, he would be shy. Or did the toddler know already that she wasn't his mother?

"Did you do as I asked?" Luca patted Charlie's back like he was the boy's father.

Amber nodded.

He stared at her for a long moment, studying her and not moving any closer. "So, you armed the bomb?" he asked. "You followed my instructions to the letter, I hope?"

She nodded.

"What did the wire harnesses look like?" he asked, but his body language was closed off and he started to turn his feet away from her, like he was thinking about running.

She could tell her game was coming to an end. "Give me Charlie." She stuck out her hands.

The boy snuggled in tighter to Luca.

"I'm not giving this boy to a stranger. There's no way." Luca turned around and started toward his truck.

"Wait, stop!" she called after him, running around him to get to the pickup before the man could disappear with Charlie.

She pressed her back against the truck. "You won't leave here with that boy."

Luca laughed at her, and for the first time since she'd met him, he sounded malicious. "You can go to hell. Whoever you are."

She reached under her shirt and drew her Glock. She put it down by her side, just showing him she meant business without endangering the baby. "I'm Amber Daniels, I work with STEALTH, the group you hired Tammy to destroy."

"Is that what you think was going on here?" Luca's gaze dropped to her gun. "You thought

I wanted to kill you and your friends, Ms. Daniels?"

She didn't quite know how to respond. "All I know is that I'm going to need to take Charlie to his father. I don't want anyone to get hurt. Not you, not me and not that baby," she said, motioning toward Charlie. "As it is, right now there are people all over in these woods who would be happy to pull the trigger and end whatever pathetic life you think you have."

"Ms. Daniels, I can see how you would make such assumptions…if you were not aware of the deal Ms. Reynolds and I had made." Luca motioned to her gun. "If you were aware, you wouldn't have that gun. Instead, you would be thanking me. I'm saving you and your friends' lives, not taking them. I've already had more than my fill of blood and guts in the name of my father."

"What does this have to do with your father?"

"Fathers have a way of forcing a son's hand, but it is up to the son to choose the direction." Luca smiled as Charlie wiggled in his arms. "My father is not a good man. He killed my fiancée, an operative with the CIA, when he found out I had fallen in love. As a result, I promised myself I would take away his greatest love—the hate he held for the STEALTH organization. Your group has been his greatest passion for several years."

"By bombing us?" she countered.

"I had no intention of killing you. If I had wanted to, I could have merely told my father about your location and this would have been taken care of long ago. As it was, I was going to wait until things were ready and then have Tammy go to her former lover. He would have been given a choice—a choice I know AJ would have taken. Now, I hope he still will."

"AJ will never let you blow up the ranch."

"Tammy and I knew there would be no easy way of talking your teams into giving up this life—we had to act a bit, we had to convince you this was the best way to move forward." There was almost a pleading tone in his voice, or perhaps it was an air of pain. "Think about it—we could stage your deaths. In essence, I was giving you all a card to start over. You can stay in the business and change your identity or you can all go your separate ways."

She felt a lump rise in her throat as she thought about AJ being free from the burden of his position. Yet, it was everything to him. AJ *was* STEALTH.

"Why did you kidnap Charlie?"

"I did no such thing," he said, aghast. "Ms. Reynolds had me watch the boy."

"This doesn't add up. How, if you weren't forcing her, did Tammy—Ms. Reynolds—come to work for you?"

"She knew the bounty that was out on the Spades' and STEALTH's heads. You may not believe this, but she still loves AJ. They weren't meant for each other, but she felt bad for not telling him about Charlie. I think she was using this good deed as a way to clear herself of any guilt about keeping the boy away. She didn't want Charlie taking up the family business... In fact, I think making sure the whole thing goes up in smoke is like her way of ensuring that her boy gets a future of his own."

Amber didn't know what to believe, or what to do. Yet, from the way Luca spoke and his body language, she didn't believe that he was lying. This was a man on a mission, a man who wanted to protect the boy who was in his arms.

"You sent a text about Charlie—you said his life depended on this meeting. You can't tell me—"

Luca shook his head. "I know you find this hard to believe, but you are seeing this all out of context. Charlie's life is in danger, but not from me. Rather, my father will stop at nothing to bring your team to their knees. If he found out about AJ's son, he would most definitely go after the boy. While we were quietly readying everything, there was no safer spot for Charlie in the world than with me. The last place my father would ever think to look."

Amber's head was spinning with all this. But she raised her hand up into the air, signaling to her teams.

"What are you doing?" Luca asked.

"I'm letting my team know that they aren't to shoot. Don't give me a reason to change my mind."

Luca smiled. "I'm glad I've convinced you."

"All you've done for now is convinced me that you have useful information and aren't worth killing...*yet*." Amber put the gun back into its holster, satisfied that she was no longer in danger. She gave the safe signal to the teams. "Give me Charlie and it will prove to me that you are telling me the truth."

Luca gave the boy a kiss to the top of his head, whispering something in Italian in the little boy's ear. "It's okay, Charlie." He lifted the boy from his hip and sat him down on the ground, taking him by the hand.

They walked toward her and he placed the little boy's winter-chilled fingers in her hand.

The boy looked up at her and sent her a toothy smile.

These Spade boys had one hell of a way of making a girl fall in love at first sight.

Epilogue

AJ sat on the beach, reading the article on his phone about a mysterious explosion at a ranch in Montana. Thirty people had been killed and it was rumored that they were an antigovernment group of some sort.

The public outcry, thanks to their little lie, had been minimal. No one cared about outliers and extremists, unless they were in their faces. As it was, the ranch had been made ready for winter and cloaked for satellites.

According to Zoey, the uppity ups in the government were happy to play along with their ruse. Everything had gone surprisingly well thanks to Luca's plan. It had taken quite a bit of convincing on his part to prove his intentions were legitimate and, though his methods were unique, in the end even Zoey had come around to his line of thinking and had helped plan their out.

It was amazing what a person could do with

a little technology and all the right friends. Blowing up a back corner of the ranch had been hard, but necessary to signal to their enemies that they were gone. Making them all virtually disappear had taken slightly more work—faking death certificates and recreating identities—but it had all been worth it in the end. Each and every one of the Spades and Martins and their families were free.

It was a hell of a feeling to not be on hit lists around the globe.

He glanced down the beach, where Zoey and her husband, Eli, were on boogie boards with their oldest child. Even from here, AJ could make out the bump of the baby that was now growing in her belly.

His thoughts moved to Tammy. He had missed so much with her, not seeing this stage of her pregnancy with Charlie, or even being there for his first steps. Thankfully, he and Amber—now officially retired, thanks to Kendra's very fine legal and negotiation skills— were making it up in true Spade fashion by showing the boy everything the world had to offer.

Admittedly, part of his desire to spoil his son was out of the guilt he would forever feel for Tammy's sacrifice. Though he would never agree with what she had done or be okay with her concealing the baby from him, in the end she had gotten what she had most wanted for their son—a stable home, one out of the line of fire and far from the world of black ops.

Tammy's autopsy had been taxing, due to the state of her remains, but the pathologists had reported that they hadn't found any arsenic in the tissues of her hand or other remains. The news had come as somewhat of a relief as he was glad she had been saved the ravages of poisoning—a poison had still played a role, though tangentially, in her death.

Her funeral had been brief, but respectful. It had been a beautiful service, and Charlie had played on the grass near the area where she had been laid to rest. Luca, as well as everyone from the Spade and Martin families, had shown up to pay their respects.

In a way, it hadn't felt like a funeral for only Tammy; rather, it felt like a dirge marking the ending of an era.

He took a long drink of his beer and let the sun soak into his skin as he stared out at the sparkling water.

"You okay?" Amber asked from beside him on the beach.

He smiled over at her. "Absolutely," he said, taking her hand in his and smiling brightly.

"Retirement is agreeing with you, baby. I

don't think I've ever seen you look so relaxed."
She brushed a bit of sand from her leg as she
smiled.

"It's a tough gig when the hardest choices I
have to make in a day are how we're going to
keep Charlie busy, what we are going to have
for dinner and then how I'm going to make love
to you at night." He lifted her hand and gave it a
quick kiss, then sent her a devilish smile.

Amber giggled. "Well, I can't wait to see
what you have in store for me tonight."

Charlie stood up with his little yellow plas-
tic shovel and toddled over to them from the
mound of sand he had created on the beach.
"Look what I built," he said, his words still
that muddled sound of a toddler.

Amber smiled over at him. "What is it,
buddy?"

"It's a dragon, Mama," Charlie said, standing up and putting his arms out. He zoomed
around flapping his arms like they were giant
wings, completely unaware of what he had
done to his father and Amber.

AJ looked over at her. Amber's eyes were
wide with excitement and there were tears
starting to form. "He's never called you that
before, has he?"

She shook her head. "You heard it, too?"

He leaned over and kissed her gently, brushing a hair off her tanned face. He turned the diamond engagement ring on her finger. "I guess it's official."

"What is, honey?" she asked, looking into his eyes and smiling brightly.

AJ gave her one more kiss to her forehead. "We have Charlie's blessing. We are a family—now and forever."

* * * * *

Get 4 FREE REWARDS!

We'll send you 2 FREE Books plus 2 FREE Mystery Gifts.

Both the **Harlequin Intrigue®** and **Harlequin® Romantic Suspense** series feature compelling novels filled with heart-racing action-packed romance that will keep you on the edge of your seat.

YES! Please send me 2 FREE novels from the Harlequin Intrigue or Harlequin Romantic Suspense series and my 2 FREE gifts (gifts are worth about $10 retail). After receiving them, if I don't wish to receive any more books, I can return the shipping statement marked "cancel." If I don't cancel, I will receive 6 brand-new Harlequin Intrigue Larger-Print books every month and be billed just $6.24 each in the U.S. or $6.74 each in Canada, a savings of at least 14% off the cover price or 4 brand-new Harlequin Romantic Suspense books every month and be billed just $5.24 each in the U.S. and $5.99 each in Canada, a savings of at least 13% off the cover price. It's quite a bargain! Shipping and handling is just 50¢ per book in the U.S. and $1.25 per book in Canada.* I understand that accepting the 2 free books and gifts places me under no obligation to buy anything. I can always return a shipment and cancel at any time by calling the number below. The free books and gifts are mine to keep no matter what I decide.

Choose one: ☐ **Harlequin Intrigue Larger-Print** (199/399 HDN GRA2) ☐ **Harlequin Romantic Suspense** (240/340 HDN GRCE)

Name (please print)

Address   Apt. #

City   State/Province   Zip/Postal Code

Email: Please check this box ☐ if you would like to receive newsletters and promotional emails from Harlequin Enterprises ULC and its affiliates. You can unsubscribe anytime.

Mail to the **Harlequin Reader Service:**
IN U.S.A.: P.O. Box 1341, Buffalo, NY 14240-8531
IN CANADA: P.O. Box 603, Fort Erie, Ontario L2A 5X3

Want to try 2 free books from another series! Call 1-800-873-8635 or visit www.ReaderService.com.

*Terms and prices subject to change without notice. Prices do not include sales taxes, which will be charged (if applicable) based on your state or country of residence. Canadian residents will be charged applicable taxes. Offer not valid in Quebec. This offer is limited to one order per household. Books received may not be as shown. Not valid for current subscribers to the Harlequin Intrigue or Harlequin Romantic Suspense series. All orders subject to approval. Credit or debit balances in a customer's account(s) may be offset by any other outstanding balance owed by or to the customer. Please allow 4 to 6 weeks for delivery. Offer available while quantities last.

Your Privacy—Your information is being collected by Harlequin Enterprises ULC, operating as Harlequin Reader Service. For a complete summary of the information we collect, how we use this information and to whom it is disclosed, please visit our privacy notice located at corporate.harlequin.com/privacy-notice. From time to time we may also exchange your personal information with reputable third parties. If you wish to opt out of this sharing of your personal information, please visit readerservice.com/consumerschoice or call 1-800-873-8635. **Notice to California Residents**—Under California law, you have specific rights to control and access your data. For more information on these rights and how to exercise them, visit corporate.harlequin.com/california-privacy.

HIHRS22R2

COUNTRY LEGACY COLLECTION

19 FREE BOOKS IN ALL!

Cowboys, adventure and romance await you in this new collection! Enjoy superb reading all year long with books by bestselling authors like Diana Palmer, Sasha Summers and Marie Ferrarella!